**"I love you, Ashley.
I want to marry you."**

Ashley had a sensation that she was being drawn into a web of words. "Michael, I can't marry you just to provide Victoria with a father."

"Why do people get married, Ashley?"

"They get married because they love each other," she said too loudly.

"Exactly!" His eyes were trained on her upturned face. "I love you. And I'm almost sure you love me. But because of what happened with David, you're scared to admit it. You think if you say 'I love you,' that I'll vanish in a puff of smoke."

"That's ridiculous!"

Damn you Michael Gault, she thought furiously. *You've got me cornered. Either I climb on the fence to balance between heaven and earth, or I call myself a coward.*

Books by Sandra Field

HARLEQUIN PRESENTS
568—WALK BY MY SIDE
639—AN ATTRACTION OF OPPOSITES
681—A MISTAKE IN IDENTITY
768—A CHANGE OF HEART
799—OUT OF WEDLOCK

writing as Jan MacLean
529—AN ISLAND LOVING

HARLEQUIN ROMANCE
1870—TO TRUST MY LOVE
2398—THE WINDS OF WINTER
2457—THE STORMS OF SPRING
2480—SIGHT OF A STRANGER
2577—THE TIDES OF SUMMER

writing as Jan MacLean
2210—TO BEGIN AGAIN
2287—BITTER HOMECOMING
2295—EARLY SUMMER
2348—WHITE FIRE
2547—ALL OUR TOMORROWS

HARLEQUIN SUPERROMANCE
writing as Jocelyn Haley
11—LOVE WILD AND FREE
31—WINDS OF DESIRE
54—SERENADE FOR A LOST LOVE
88—CRY OF THE FALCON
122—SHADOWS IN THE SUN

These books may be available at your local bookseller.

Don't miss any of our special offers. Write to us at the following address for information on our newest releases.

Harlequin Reader Service
P.O. Box 52040, Phoenix, AZ 85072-2040
Canadian address: P.O. Box 2800, Postal Station A,
5170 Yonge St., Willowdale, Ont. M2N 6J3

SANDRA FIELD

out of wedlock

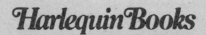

TORONTO • NEW YORK • LONDON
AMSTERDAM • PARIS • SYDNEY • HAMBURG
STOCKHOLM • ATHENS • TOKYO • MILAN

With thanks to Don Deal

———————•———————

Harlequin Presents first edition July 1985
ISBN 0-373-10799-4

Original hardcover edition published in 1985
by Mills & Boon Limited

CHAPTER ONE

The sleek black Mercedes raced silently through the darkness . . .

The man at the wheel, whose name was Michael Gault, smiled ironically to himself. *Nice sentence*, he thought. *Too bad it isn't true. Mind you, it is dark, that's accurate enough. And I am driving a Mercedes.*

He had reached a ten-mile stretch in the road where the forest pressed to the ditches, black and impenetrable, seemingly held back only by the regularly spaced telephone poles and the narrow wire strung between them. No houses, no lights, no people. Not even any other cars. It was raining, too, the wind driving the drops against the windshield.

The headlights lit up the incline ahead of him. As he pressed on the accelerator, the engine backfired and the speedometer wavered from ninety kilometres an hour to eighty to seventy. Irritably he shoved his foot to the floor. Bucking and spitting, the Mercedes lurched up the hill.

It was incredible what rude noises such an elegant car could make, Michael decided. Whatever the problem was, it was getting worse. The Mercedes was losing power steadily, and the only time the motor ran with even a semblance of its normal well-bred smoothness was on the downhill slopes. *Damn the car, anyway.* He hated to think how many thousands of dollars were represented by the gleaming metal body, the exquisitely comfortable leather upholstery, the mysterious array of dials on the dashboard. More than he would ever pay for a car, that he did know. His old jeep would have worked better than this, even with the leaky radiator. After all, it hadn't been leaking very badly. And it was his jeep he would be driving if Mary hadn't insisted he borrow her Mercedes rather than risk an overheated engine.

Damn Mary, too, he added for good measure, choosing to ignore that as she had handed him the keys after the board meeting she had murmured something about the motor not running as smoothly as it should. She'd probably assumed he could fix it. That was the trouble with women—just because you were a man, they expected you to be able to take an engine apart and put it together again in working order. Well, in this particular case Mary had got the wrong man.

In a series of vulgar hiccoughs the Mercedes made it to the crest of another hill. Michael Gault peered through the windshield, not sure exactly where he was, for he had only used this road once or twice before, preferring the more travelled route to the east. But unless he was mistaken, there should be a village in a couple of miles. He'd stopped there for gas once this summer when he was driving the jeep; the reason he remembered was because the lad on the gas pumps had been silent to the point of surliness, as far from the prototype for the friendly and hospitable Maritimer of the tourist ads as anyone could be.

However, tonight he wasn't in a position to be choosy. If he was lucky—and his thoughts were punctuated by a volley of backfires that made the car shudder like a machine gun—he'd make it as far as the gas station before the damn thing died on him and left him marooned in the middle of nowhere. Provided the place was open; it must be nearly ten o'clock.

It was considerably more than a couple of miles before the first lights of the village twinkled through the rain and the darkness, and a green sign announced that he was in Lower Hampton. It was a typical Nova Scotian rural community, made up of vinyl-sided bungalows and shingled older houses, with the usual white-turreted church and a little cluster of stores and businesses. The red, white and blue gas station sign was still illuminated. The Mercedes crept into the paved yard like a very old man, coming to a halt by the garage door with a feeble wheeze.

Leaving the motor running, Michael Gault got out, automatically stretching the stiffness from his bad knee. Although he could not see anyone, the lights were shining from within the garage. Frowning slightly, he pushed open the glass door into the office and stepped inside.

The cash register rested on top of the counter, while neat rows of candy bars and potato chips were arranged under it. A pop machine stood in one corner. Like oversized rubber bands, an array of fan-belts hung from the ceiling; on the shelves, tidily aligned, were containers of antifreeze, motor oil, brake fluid, and lubricant.

Michael had spent too many years dependent on his eye for detail for his very survival to be unaware of the almost excessive tidiness of the room: floor swept, ashtray clean, wastebasket empty. The other thing that struck him was the music, which was presumably coming from a radio in the garage. It was not the rock music or Country and Western that he might have expected. It was, unless he was mistaken, one of Haydn's London symphonies.

The sign over the door that led into the garage proper said Employees Only. Disregarding it, he stepped down the two cement stairs and looked around him.

The first thing he saw was a pair of scuffed, steel-toed boots. They were attached to dungareed legs, the legs disappearing under a jacked-up light blue car that had seen better days, for its body was pitted with rust and the rear headlight had obviously collided with something harder than itself in the recent past.

As Michael Gault cleared his throat, the violins joined forces in a crescendo. The boots did not move. A single plaintive flute replaced the violins. He said hopefully, 'Excuse me, please. I've got car trouble.'

The boots gave a startled jerk. The legs emerged from

under the car followed by the body on a wooden-wheeled platform, and finally by the head. The man's smile faded. It was the same boy who had served him this summer, the silent one. Not much chance of getting the Mercedes fixed here. What in hell was he going to do?

The lad rolled off the creeper and stood up. He was wearing grease-stained overalls over a dark sweater, a khaki woollen hat pulled down over his ears. There was more grease on his face, streaking the straight nose. His eyes were grey, and guarded. 'Can I help you?' he said. His voice was light, high-pitched, his cheeks and small determined chin innocent of a beard.

The sudden movement unexpectedly swift, the man reached over and tweaked the khaki hat from the boy's head. Under the hat was a swath of pinned-up hair, pale as summer wheat.

Ashley MacCulloch glared at the man. 'What did you do that for?'

'I thought for a minute you were a boy.'

'Well, I'm not. As you can see.'

'Why the masquerade?'

She shoved her hands in the pockets of her shapeless overalls. 'Hardly a masquerade. Would you suggest I wear a dress instead? That *would* look cute!'

In a leisurely fashion Michael surveyed her from the scuffed toes of her boots to the crown of pale, shining hair. 'You're right—it probably would.'

'I didn't mean it that way! I meant I couldn't very well fix cars dressed in frills and lace.'

'*You* fix cars?'

Here we go again, thought Ashley, nettled. 'A woman is just as capable of fixing a car as a man is,' she said crossly.

'You wouldn't be strong enough.'

'I don't do it with my bare hands. I use tools—have you ever heard of them? Wonderful inventions.'

'Are you always this rude to your customers?' he asked coldly.

'Only when they insult me first,' she retorted. Colour tinged her cheeks and her grey eyes were turbulent; she did not look at all like a boy. 'If you want to see my credentials, they're over there.' She indicated two framed certificates hanging on the far wall.

'I never did place much faith in bits of paper. Why don't we see if you can fix my car instead??'

'What's wrong with it?'

'If I knew that, I wouldn't be here. Because just as you are something of a rarity, so, unfortunately, am I—an adult male who knows nothing about what goes on under the hood of a car, and couldn't care less.' He finished his statement by giving her a sudden, disarming smile.

Ashley caught her breath, for his smile lit up his face. Although he was over average height, her initial impression had been one of ordinariness: brown hair, regular features, a face that would fade into a crowd and never be missed. But his smile brought attention to his well-shaped mouth and the strength in his jaw; and his eyes, she thought with an odd reluctance, were far from ordinary. They were blue, the same deep blue as the delphiniums that her grandfather had grown in the garden behind the garage this past summer. Which was not a very appropriate simile, for there was nothing remotely effeminate about the man.

The eyes that she was so busy admiring were still patiently trained on her face. Flustered, she said, 'Where's your car?' *Intelligent question, Ashley. Go to the top of the class.*

'Outside in the rain. Unless I was fortunate enough to have it stolen.'

'Around here that's always a possibility,' was the dry response. Trying hard to take command of the situation, she added, 'I'll open the door and you can drive in over the lift.'

She hauled on the chain and the panelled door slid upwards on its tracks. Ducking, the man hurried out into the rain. A car door slammed, and then he was steering a shiny black Mercedes over the pneumatic hoist. Ashley let the door back down, and with the speed of long practice attached corrugated rubber tubing between the exhaust pipe and a circular vent in the door, to avoid the danger of exhaust fumes with their deadly carbon monoxide content. Only then did she take a look at the car.

It was a 280 S. Probably eight or nine years old, she decided, its body in excellent condition. Six-cylinder, gasoline-powered. She'd never worked on one before; after all her fine words, it would be humiliating if she couldn't locate the source of the trouble.

The man had rolled down the window. 'Shall I turn it off?'

'Not yet,' she answered coolly. 'It's running very unevenly, isn't it?'

He gave her a pungent description of the car's behaviour, to which she listened carefully, keeping a straight face with difficulty. 'Has this only been happening since you filled the tank?' she asked.

'I have no idea. The car belongs to a friend.'

Even as he spoke, Ashley noticed a pair of women's gloves carelessly flung on the dash, brown pigskin gloves, as expensive in their own way as the car was. To her horror, for she had only meant to think the words, not say them, she heard herself blurt, 'She must be a very good friend. A new Mercedes this size retails for over forty thousand dollars.'

The vivid eyes narrowed. 'That, my dear, need not concern you. Just make it work so I can get on my way, will you?'

She bit her lip mutinously, knowing she had deserved the reprimand, yet liking it not at all. 'Open the hood, will you, please?' she said stiffly, forcing herself to concentrate on her job. It could be water in the gasoline, or a leaking fuel line; however, there was no noticeable odour of gasoline. She'd check the wiring first and go from there. Bending to her task, she felt the familiar kindling of interest, the excitement that always came when she had to diagnose the cause of a problem, no matter what the make of the car. Listen to the symptoms, run through the possible list of causes, and check them out: a basic plan that rarely failed her.

This time she was lucky. She noticed the bad ignition wire almost immediately, and followed it to the coil, removing the rubber cap. Straightening, she called out, 'Put the car in drive with the brake on, and then accelerate—I want around two thousand rpm.' She gave a tiny sound of satisfaction as he obeyed her, for the coil arced, the flash showing a thin jagged crack in the tower. 'Okay, that's enough!'

Replacing the cap, Ashley walked back to the window. 'You've got a cracked coil.'

'So what does that mean?' he said warily.

'It means you'll have to get a new one. I can order it from Halifax first thing tomorrow morning and it'll come in on the afternoon bus. It's only half an hour's work at the most to replace it.' She added critically, 'The front left tire is low on air, too. Your friend doesn't take very good care of her car.'

'Let's leave my friend out of this,' he said with dangerous calm. 'Are you saying you can't fix this crate until tomorrow?'

'That's right. Although it's hardly a crate.'

'I've got another forty miles to reach home. Just how am I supposed to get there—walk?'

'You certainly can't drive your car.' She added without much conviction, 'Maybe I can find someone to drive you.'

'At ten-thirty at night? In the middle of a rainstorm?'

He was right, of course. Nonplussed, Ashley stared at him. He had turned off the motor and now got out of the car, towering over her. He was wearing dark-coloured cords and a lumberman's jacket over a black sweater, clothes that told her nothing about him, for they could have been bought off the rack in any number of places and were without any particular distinction. How strange it was, therefore, that she should sense behind this undistinguished exterior the force of a personality that was highly individualistic. '*I* don't know what you're going to do,' she said in exasperation.

'Go to the nearest motel, I guess.'

'The nearest motel belongs to the Macallums, three miles up the road. They left for Florida last week.'

'Then what's the second nearest?'

'There's no need to shout,' she said coldly. 'There isn't another one.'

'A guest house? A rooming house? A nice elderly widow who takes in strangers who have nowhere else to go?'

'No, no, and no. This is Lower Hampton, not Halifax. No one ever stops here, they just drive through.'

'I can see why,' he said grimly. 'Next time remind me to do the same. I'm going to be bloody uncomfortable sleeping in the back seat of the car.'

Her eyes widened. Without thinking, she said, 'You can't do that. You'll have to stay at the house.' And regretted the words almost immediately.

'Whose house?'

'My grandfather's—I live with him. It's the house next to the gas station.' Grandad, unlike most people, would be delighted when she arrived home with a complete stranger in tow.

There was a peculiar note in the man's voice. 'You're offering me a bed in your house? But you don't even know me.'

She grimaced at him. 'What else am I supposed to do? It's October, after all—I can't leave you to sleep out here.'

'I might be a murderer. Or a rapist.'

'You don't look like either one.'

'Like most of the general public, your image of a murderer is someone who runs around slavering at the jaw, red in tooth and nail. Most of them are very ordinary people, believe me.'

Ashley wanted to ask how he knew. Instead she said, a wry smile pulling at her mouth, 'Whatever the case, I don't think you're one.'

'You're much too trusting.'

Something flickered in her eyes and the smile vanished. 'Do you or do you not want to stay at the house?'

He said abruptly, 'I don't even know your name.'

'Ashley MacCulloch.'

'Ashley . . . that's far too gentle a name for you.' He tilted his head. 'You should be a Cynthia or a Becky, something sharp and prickly. Ashley sounds like a sigh on the wind.'

'Now who's being rude?' Quickly she turned away, lowering the hood of the Mercedes, wondering why a stranger's words should have so much power to wound.

There was a tiny silence. Then she felt a hand drop on her shoulder. She tensed, wishing he would let go. 'Look at me,' he said, and unwillingly she raised her eyes to his. 'I'm sorry,' he went on. 'I was being facetious, and I hurt you, didn't I?'

She moved back a couple of steps so that his hand fell to his side; if she had learned one lesson over the past year and a half, it was to hide her feelings. 'I happen to like my name, that's all . . . You haven't told me yours.'

'Michael Gault.'

She nodded an acknowledgment, not bothering to smile. 'I'm going to lock the garage now. Then we'll go over to the house.'

'I did apologise, Ashley MacCulloch.'

A certain note in his voice brought her up short, and again she had the impression of a forcible personality behind the regular features. 'I'm aware of that,' she said brusquely. 'What do you want—a medal?'

'By the look of you, you'd stick it in rather than pin it on. Do you dislike all men on general principles, or is there something about me that rubs you the wrong way?'

Glowering, she decided she'd been a fool to invite him to the house. It wouldn't have hurt him to have spent the night in his car; he was a man well used to looking after himself, she was sure. 'Look, it's been a long day, it's past closing time, and I'm tired,' she said, stripping off thin surgical gloves as she spoke and dropping them in the oil drum that served as a garbage container; the gloves kept the worst of the grease from her hands. She squirted liquid cleaner on her fingers and massaged them thoroughly, before rinsing them off with the hose that was looped against the wall.

'Once you've answered the question, we can leave.'

He had not raised his voice, and his pose as he leaned against the Mercedes was completely relaxed, but somehow Ashley was not deceived. 'Are you threatening me?' she said sharply.

'God forbid. I'm merely expecting from you a modicum of good manners.'

'Oh, do forgive me,' she said with heavy irony. 'I've spent too much time in the backwoods, obviously. Let me tell you something, Mr Gault. If I'd been at all interested in men before I came to Lower Hampton, I certainly wouldn't be now. Half the guys who come to the gas station are enough to put any woman off the male of the species—permanently.'

'Then why don't you include me in the other half?' he asked blandly.

Quite suddenly Ashley had had enough of their verbal fencing. 'I'm not sure where I'd put you,' she said with complete honesty, drying her hands on some paper towel before locking the two big doors. 'Do you need anything out of the car?'

'No, thanks.' He followed her into the office. 'By the way, I like your taste in music.'

'My grandfather hates the radio—says it's nothing but commercials and hockey scores. He's not overly fond of classical music, either. So I tend to do most of my listening in the garage.'

'Do you always work alone here after dark?'

'Grandad's just next door,' she answered impatiently, locking the cash register and setting the burglar alarm. 'After you.'

'In other words, why don't I mind my own business?'

'Exactly.'

He stepped out into the rain, the wind stirring his hair as she secured the door. 'If the neighbourhood's that tough, it doesn't seem like a very smart thing to do.'

'There's really no choice,' she responded shortly. 'Let's run for the house or we'll be soaked.'

It was a small white clapboard house of no particular architectural distinction; it was, however, freshly painted, red trim around the doors and windows. The flowerbeds were cleaned up for winter and the lawn raked clean of fallen leaves. Ashley ran ahead, feeling the rain cool on her face, and opened the side door. Looking back over her shoulder, she saw to her surprise that she had covered the ground much more rapidly than the stranger; and saw the reason immediately. He was favouring his right knee, his run an awkward lopsided shamble. It shocked her, for it did not go with the lean, loose-knit body. Ushering him in, she said without finesse, 'Did you hurt your leg recently?'

'Nearly three years ago.'

'That long ago?'

'Yeah . . . it'll never get any better than it is now.'

Something in his voice forbade further questions. 'Oh. I'm sorry.'

The cold night air had brought colour to her cheeks; as she bent to unlace her boots, a heavy strand of hair fell free of its pins, shining like pale gold under the light. Standing her boots neatly on the rubber tray, Ashley straightened, to find Michael Gault staring at her fixedly, his expression unreadable. 'What's the matter?' she said. 'Shouldn't I have asked about your leg?'

'It's not that. It's just that you make a much better-looking girl than a boy.'

Ashley had been about to unzip her overalls. Willing herself not to blush, she murmured, 'How gallant of you,' and slid down the zipper, stepping out of the overalls and hanging them up. Then she pulled her dark sweater over her head, which further disarranged her hair, and slung the sweater over the same hanger. She was wearing faded, tight-fitting jeans and a much-washed T-shirt that clung to the fullness of her breasts.

He said calmly, '*Much* better-looking. It's a pity you don't like men.'

'I make an exception for my grandfather,' she replied sweetly, raising her voice to call, 'Grandad! Are you still up? . . . Do come in, Mr Gault.'

The back porch led into the kitchen, which was dominated by an old-fashioned wood stove that sent a warm glow around the room. The wallpaper, Ashley's choice, was a charming design of flowering herbs, complemented by the ruffled green curtains and the green cushions on the two old-fashioned rocking chairs; against one wall stood a playpen with a collection of brightly coloured toys, while a high chair was pulled up to the pine table.

His carpet slippers shuffling on the floor, Ashley's grandfather came into the room just as Ashley was hanging the garage keys on a hook by the door.

'Grandad, this is Michael Gault,' she said hurriedly. 'His car's broken down and I can't get the part until tomorrow. Do you mind if he stays overnight? He can have my room.'

Matthew Stewart gave the stranger a level stare from under shaggy white eyebrows, a scrutiny Michael Gault met with admirable aplomb. Then the old man stuck out his hand. 'How do? No night for a breakdown. Where do you hail from?'

'Starr River.'

'Too far to walk. In the lumber business?'

'I own a sheep farm there.'

'That so? You the city feller who bought old Abe

Knudsen's place a year or so back?' Michael Gault nodded. 'How's it going? You making a buck?'

'Grandad!' Ashley protested, knowing from long experience that Matthew's insatiable curiosity was only equalled by his lack of tact, and that his zest for living involved gleaning as many intimate details as he could about everyone who lived within a hundred-mile radius.

Injured, Matthew expostulated, 'I was only asking, Ashley.'

'Why don't you ask him if he'd like a cup of tea instead?'

'Women . . .' Matthew sighed. 'You married, son?'

Michael Gault grinned. 'No, sir.'

'Smart man.' Matthew's nostrils quivered with interest. 'Why not?'

'Grandad——'

'Up until the last year or so I never had the time,' Michael interrupted imperturbably. 'However, that could change.'

It was not coincidence that the sleek black Mercedes and the expensive pigskin gloves should flicker across Ashley's mind. She said nastily, 'He's going to marry money, Grandad.'

'How do you know that?'

'An educated guess. Mr Gault——'

'The name is Michael.'

She compressed her lips. 'Can I get you some tea or coffee?'

'Tea would be fine, thank you.'

'And put out some of that chocolate cake, Ashley,' her grandfather interjected. 'The man looks hungry.'

Ashley busied herself in the pantry, glad of the excuse to leave the room, for there was something about their visitor that brought out the worst in her. She must try and behave in a more civilised fashion, or else Matthew, who knew her well, would draw all the wrong conclusions. Contrary to herself, Matthew was enjoying himself enormously. That, after all, was why she had invited Michael Gault to stay, wasn't it?

Deciding not to pursue that question any further, she put out cups and saucers and cut generous wedges of the chocolate cake, all her movements neat and quick. Back in the kitchen she found the two men deep in a discussion of North Country Cheviots, Suffolks, and Corriedales, and was not at all surprised that Matthew should be knowledgeable about all three breeds of sheep; at the age of seventy-two he still read voraciously, loading his arms with books about everything from bee-keeping to Swiss banks on the monthly visits of the bookmobile. It was plain that their visitor was also enjoying himself. Helping himself to a large piece of cake, he gestured with it as he defended his preference for Cheviots, his singularly attractive smile being bestowed upon her grandfather far more frequently than it had been on her.

Ashley sat quietly, sipping her tea, watching her grandfather with affection. His hair was as white and unruly as his eyebrows, while his eyes were sea-blue and somehow innocent, like those of a child. His wool trousers were brown, his checked shirt green and red, and his patched sweater an unsubtle shade of mustard yellow, for Matthew found life too short to worry about minor details like clothes. He argued, laughed, ate, and drank with gusto, and some days his immoderate enthusiasm for the business of living nearly drove Ashley crazy; but next to Victoria, she loved him more than anyone else in the world.

The talk had moved to the hazards of lambing season, and almost reluctantly Ashley shifted her attention back to Michael Gault. She guessed him to be in his mid-thirties, and as she watched the play of expression on his face wondered how she had ever thought him ordinary. On the contrary, he was extremely attractive with his lean, well-kept hands and deep voice, his long-limbed body and astonishingly blue eyes. He was also holding his own with her grandfather: no mean feat.

Restlessly she got up, refilling the men's cups, then

leaving the room and running upstairs. Because they had no guest room, she would have to sleep on the cot in Victoria's room and give the visitor her bed, which meant she must change the sheets and tidy up a bit. Not that her bedroom was untidy. She had spent over a year in her grandfather's house now, and this room had come to represent home for her in a way the fussily feminine room in her parents' house never had. In this room she had laughed and wept, had raged and despaired; it was here she had felt the first pangs of labour, and to this room that she had brought home her tiny daughter Victoria only six months ago. Letting her eyes linger on the plain blue curtains, the hand-stitched quilt, the well-stocked bookshelves, she recognised how much of her growing up had been done in this room. And for most of it, she had her grandfather to thank . . .

Giving herself a little shake, she put fresh blue sheets on the bed, and removed her toilet articles from the white-painted dresser as well as her housecoat and nightdress from the closet. After putting clean towels on the chair, she turned on the bedside lamp and drew the curtains.

The rain was drumming on the roof and dripping from the gutters. She couldn't have allowed Mike Gault to sleep in his car tonight, not in this weather; yet as she looked around the cosy, unpretentious little room she was suddenly afraid. It was her haven, her sanctuary, a very private place. Why then was she allowing a stranger to invade it? It would be his body in the white spool bed, his head on the pillow where hers belonged in the most intimate invasion of all. She shivered, remembering David, and hugged her arms across her breast. That was over, done with . . . there was no need to remember it.

Leaving the room, she put more clean towels in the bathroom, and went downstairs. When she re-entered the kitchen, Michael Gault was on the telephone, and she couldn't help overhearing the last of his conversation. '. . . and Tim's behaved himself, has he? . . . Good. Okay, Beth, I should be home by late tomorrow afternoon. Call me here if there's any problem. Goodbye.'

Who was Beth? Not his wife, for he had said he wasn't married. And who was Tim? Hoping her curiosity didn't show in her face, Ashley watched Michael replace the receiver on the hook.

'Thanks, Matthew,' he said easily. 'They'd be expecting me home by now, I wouldn't want them to worry.'

Her grandfather gave an exaggerated yawn. 'Well now, guess I'll head for bed. An old fellow like me needs his sleep. Good night, Michael, hope you'll rest comfortably. 'Night, Ashley.' He kissed her on the forehead, his moustache tickling her skin, a sensation she remembered since childhood.

She knew very well he was purposely leaving her and Michael Gault alone together. Her grandfather rarely went to bed early when they had a visitor, for he thrived on company and could stay up half the night when he had a mind to. She said limpidly, 'I'm going up myself, Grandad, I'm tired. Did you lock up?'

'I did that. Now don't you neglect our visitor, Ashley, that wouldn't be polite.'

'I have to open the garage at eight tomorrow,' she replied pointedly. 'Tommy can't come, he's got the 'flu.' Tommy was the seventeen-year-old high school dropout who looked after the gas pumps for them, leaving Ashley free for the mechanical work.

'In my day you didn't stay away from work because of a bit of sickness,' Matthew said grumpily. 'Pour yourself another cup of tea, girl, and relax. G'night, all.'

As he shuffled out of the room, closing the door behind him, Ashley pulled a rude face at his back. 'He's a manipulator,' she said crossly. 'He needs far less sleep than I do.'

'I see . . . so what's he hoping to accomplish by leaving you and me together?'

'Heaven knows,' she replied, less than truthfully, somehow not at all surprised that their visitor should see through Matthew's stratagem.

'He was pretty quick to ask me if I was married.'

You asked for it. . . . 'Grandad is an inverterate matchmaker who doesn't get many opportunities as far as I'm concerned. Don't pay any attention to him.' She gave Michael Gault a perfunctory smile. 'I'm going to bed. I left the light on in your room. The bathroom's across the hall.'

'Hold it a minute.' His words had that unconscious note of authority that she had noticed before; its effect was to make her raise her chin defiantly, a move he ignored. 'I gather I'm putting you out of your bed,' he went on. 'Can't I sleep on the couch downstairs?'

She had already noticed that in her socked feet she was at least six inches shorter than he. 'I hardly fit on the couch, so I'm sure you wouldn't.' She stared absorbedly at her fingers, knowing she might as well tell him before he asked; he must have seen the playpen and the toys. 'It's no problem. There's a cot in my daughter's room, I'll sleep there.'

After an instant's silence he said, 'So it is your child. I figured it had to be.'

'Yes.' She braced herself, knowing what was coming next, somehow unable to forestall him, quite unaware of the beleaguered look in her eyes and the defensiveness of her posture.

He reached over, taking her left hand in his and smoothing the skin on her ringless fingers. She suffered his touch, her whole body poised for flight. 'No one's mentioned a husband. Does he live here, too?'

'No.'

'Are you divorced?'

'I've never been married.' There it was out.

'. . . I see.'

There was nothing in the two little words to give her a clue to his feelings. Across her mind's eye flashed the faces from the past with their various reactions: David's stunned look, her mother's tears, her father's disbelief and raw contempt; and, more recently, the open disdain of some of her neighbours in Lower Hampton and the lewd comments of the lumber crews. Avoiding Michael Gault's eyes, she mumbled, 'Do you need anything before you go upstairs?'

'A smile, maybe?'

Startled, her lashes flickered up. 'Why should you care whether I smile or not?'

'You look better when you smile. Most people do.'

She said slowly, 'You're a very strange man.'

'What were you expecting? That I'd faint with horror when you told me you had a child born out of wedlock? Come off it, Ashley. These are the nineteen-eighties, not the Victorian era.'

'I'm not sure the nineteen-eighties have arrived in Lower Hampton.'

'That's quite possible. You could always move somewhere more progressive.'

'I can't. Grandad wouldn't want to move. And I have to work.'

'Then stop going around apologising for yourself.'

His words flicked her on the raw. 'You don't have the remotest understanding of what my life is like,' she snapped. 'So keep your facile solutions to yourself.'

'You'd rather wallow in misery, is that it?'

'I *don't*!'

'I've only seen you twice, Ashley MacCulloch, and each time——'

'Twice?' she interrupted.

'I stopped here for gas once this summer. Late August, maybe. I don't think you said more than two words to me.'

She had no recollection of the event at all. 'I must have had something on my mind,' she said dismissively. 'I'm going to bed. I have to be up early tomorrow to open the garage. But don't feel you have to get up when I do.'

'In other words, you'd rather I didn't.'

'It's entirely up to you,' she said dulcetly. 'I wouldn't dream of trying to influence you.'

'Oh, yes, you would, Becky-Cynthia.'

'My name is Ashley!'

'An Ashley would have played this whole scene quite differently. More like this ... give me your hand.' Somehow she found herself obeying him. 'Now smile up at me and say with at least a minimal degree of sincerity, *Good night, Michael. I hope you'll sleep well.*'

His fingers had curved around her hand, holding it firmly. Just as firmly, his eyes held hers captive. 'This is ridiculous!' she spluttered.

'Come on, Ashley, try it—I dare you. You'll be surprised—it won't hurt at all.'

He would not let go until she had complied; that she knew. Irresistibly her mind moved backwards in time, for Michael Gault reminded her of Bob, by far the favourite of her four brothers. Just so had Bob dared her to walk the top of the garden fence many years ago, coaxing her until she had wavered all the way from the old apple tree to the shed; she had fallen only when her mother had shrieked in horror from the bedroom window. Bob had picked her up and brushed the dirt from her grazed knees; Bob had been proud that she hadn't cried, either then or later during the inevitable spanking. ... That wayward little girl had had little chance to surface the last year or so, thought Ashley, feeling Michael Gault's blue eyes pull her into their depths. Perhaps it was time she reappeared.

Very deliberately, she moved closer, kissed him on the cheek and then stepped back, repeating his own words. 'Good night, Michael. I hope you'll sleep well.'

With the utmost gravity he responded. 'Thank you, Ashley. I'm sure I shall.'

There was a pause. He had released her hand; she had no idea what he was thinking. As for herself, she was already wondering what had prompted her to behave so atypically. 'If you're going up now, I'll turn out the lights,' she muttered.

'All right,' he said politely.

She closed the damper on the stove and switched off the kitchen light. Michael seemed much larger in the semi-darkness. Not looking at him, she preceded him into the narrow hallway and up the stairs. The door to her grandfather's room at the end of the hall was firmly closed. Indicating the lighted doorway to her bedroom, she said awkwardly, 'I put the towels out for you. The bathroom's the door on the left. I leave a night-light on in the hall because of the baby.'

All he said was, 'Thanks, Ashley,' but once again his smile caught at her throat, so genuine and unforced was it. She gave him a stiff little nod of acknowledgment and turned away, going into Victoria's room and closing the door.

Victoria was lying on her stomach, eyes tight shut, her whole being concentrated on the act of sleep. Her hair was as dark as Ashley's was fair; she resembled David no more than she resembled Ashley, something for which her mother had always been grateful. Dropping a quick kiss on the child's head, Ashley undressed, pulled on a nightgown, and slid into the narrow little bed, shivering at the chill between the cotton sheets. Firmly closing her mind to all that had happened that evening, she just as firmly closed her eyes. With a suddenness that was habitual, she fell asleep.

CHAPTER TWO

VICTORIA was crying. Ashley sat up in bed, rubbing dazedly at her eyes, confused because she was in the wrong room. Three forty-five ... *oh, no*! She tumbled out of bed and picked the child up, and the wail subsided to a whimper. A couple of weeks ago Victoria had started teething, her tiny gums so red and angry-looking that Ashley could hardly blame her for waking in the night; not for the first time she decided some better method should have been invented for the emergence of teeth.

She padded downstairs, changed the baby's diaper with the speed of much practice while the bottle warmed, and then sat in one of the rocking chairs to feed her. Eventually Victoria's dark lashes drifted to her cheeks and her pudgy fists relaxed. In one of those sudden rushes of protectiveness and love that could overcome Ashley at any time, she bent her head and kissed the baby's forehead, inhaling the familiar mingled scent of shampoo, clean skin, and warm milk that made up for all the busy days and disturbed nights.

'She's a beautiful child.'

Ashley jumped. 'I didn't hear you come down.'

'I should hope not,' Michael said obscurely. 'Do you have to get up every night?'

He was leaning against the doorpost as he spoke. He was wearing only the dark blue cords he had had on earlier, his chest and feet bare. Her brothers had been in the habit of wandering around the house half-dressed, much against her mother's wishes, and certainly Ashley had seen more of David than she was now seeing of Michael Gault. Why then did she feel as if she had never seen a man's body before? 'Not usually, no,' she faltered. 'But she's teething. I'm sorry she woke you.'

'I'm a light sleeper. Particularly in a strange place.'

It was an innocent enough exchange of words, Ashley thought wildly. There was no reason for her heartbeat to quicken and her cheeks to warm. No reason at all. She stood up abruptly and Victoria's blanket fell to the floor.

'I'll get it.' He bent and picked it up, standing very close to Ashley. 'Here, give me the baby while you tidy up.'

'Oh, no, I——'

'Come on, Ashley. I promise I won't drop her.'

At a loss, Ashley gazed up at him. In the soft lamplight his face was shadowed, his eyes much darker ... like the sky at dusk, she thought with a tiny quiver of her nerves. Trying to hold on to reality, she said over-loudly, 'She needs to be burped.'

'How do I do that?'

Very carefully Ashley put the baby in his arms so that the tiny dark head flopped against his shoulder. 'Pat her back, or rub it—that should do the trick.' She turned away, cleaning up the towels, the powder and vaseline, and the saucepan in which she had heated the milk. As the water gurgled down the drain, Victoria gave a juicy belch, one that would not have disgraced a two-hundred-pound beer-swilling lumberjack.

Ashley was used to her daughter's indelicacy. Even so, she turned around, a smile on her lips. Michael was grinning delightedly, his big hands cradling the child's body as he gazed down at her dark-fringed lashes and chubby pink cheeks, for Victoria, oblivious to the fuss, was fast asleep. She looked very small against the breadth of Michael's chest, very helpless. The man, his head bent, his face gentle, looked paradoxically both tender and tough, capable of love and yet also of the fiercest protection of the child in his arms.

As if a knife blade had pierced the soft flesh between her ribs, Ashley felt pain rip through her heart. David, the child's father, had never held Victoria in his arms. Had never even seen her. It should have been David standing in the kitchen holding their child, not a blue-

eyed stranger who within a few hours would be gone
from her life as if he had never been.

Michael had looked up. He could not have missed
the anguish in Ashley's features, the strained way her
hands were clasped at her breast. 'What's wrong?' he
said sharply. 'Do you want her back?'

'I—no.' She bent her head, fighting back the tears
that threatened to drown her if she ever let them start.

He crossed the room in three quick strides. 'Ashley,
tell me what's wrong.'

'I can't. It's nothing,' she said incoherently. 'I must
put her back to bed. It's *nothing*, I tell you!'

He turned away and with infinite gentleness put the
sleeping child in the armchair. Then he straightened and
walked back to Ashley, taking her shoulders in his
hands. Her nightgown was of flowered flannelette, high-
necked, long-sleeved, edged with ruffles and lace. It was
not a sexy garment. Yet it emphasised the narrowness
of her shoulders and the fragility of her hands and feet.
Her hair, straight and thick and very fair, hung down
her back, seemingly too heavy for so slender a neck.

Ashley felt the warmth of his hands seep through the
fabric of her nightgown. For a crazy moment she
longed to rest her forehead on his shoulder where
Victoria's head had rested, and fall asleep as the child
had done, knowing she was safe and cared for. How
heavenly that would be . . . and how impossible. A year
ago she had looked to David for that care, and he had
failed her utterly. When she had turned to her parents,
they too had rejected her. So she had learned to stand
alone, dimly sensing that self-reliance was the only true
safety there was. She must be more tired now than she
realised if she was tempted even momentarily to abandon
the independence she had fought so hard to achieve.

She looked up. In a brittle voice she said, 'What's
this? The inevitable pass?'

His jaw hardened. 'Just what do you mean by that?'

'Don't tell me you don't know what a pass is? I'm sure
you've made a few in your life.'

'I had no intention of making a pass at you——'

'Come off it,' she railed. 'I'm an unwed mother, remember? Which by definition means I'm easy. Cheap. Loose.' Viciously she mimicked a remark she had overheard at the gas pump. 'If she'll do it once, she'll do it again.'

If she had expected him to yell back at her, she was to be disappointed. He said drily, flicking a glance over her primly ruffled nightgown, 'You don't fit the stereotype of a loose woman, Ashley.'

'Then take your hands off me!'

'Nor do you look the least bit easy,' he drawled, paying no attention to her request. 'In fact, you look as if you'd bash my head in given the slightest chance.'

He still had not raised his voice. Baffled, she repeated stonily, 'I asked you to take your hands off me.'

'When I'm ready to.'

Her breath hissed between her teeth. A moment ago her anger had been as much directed at herself for her temporary weakness as towards him. But now it had shifted focus: the conflict had become an open clash of wills between the two of them. Biting off her words, she said, 'Let go of me.'

Michael smiled lazily. 'For a young woman who was obviously properly brought up, your manners are deplorable . . . I may have mentioned that before.'

'If you think I'm going to beg, you're mistaken!'

'One "please" will be sufficient.'

The little girl who had balanced precariously on top of the fence had reappeared earlier in the evening; now another Ashley came to the fore, perhaps a couple of years older, a blonde-haired, pigtailed child in a pretty pink dress, who had flung herself at two bigger boys who had been pummelling her brother Bob to the ground. Her mother had been scandalised when she had arrived home with her dress torn and her nose bloodied; but a week of evenings spent in her room had been worth the knowledge that she had deflected the two bullies long enough for both her and Bob to make good their escape. That little girl had been smothered lately, too. But there was no reason why she should not be resurrected . . .

Ashley threw herself sideways, kicking out at Michael with her bare feet. The undignified scuffle that followed was characterised more by its brevity than by any skill on her part. It ended with her pinned against the wall, totally immobilised, and with no very clear idea of how she had arrived there.

She gasped indignantly, 'You're a dirty fighter!'

'You started it. And what you did wasn't exactly cricket. That was my bad leg you tried to kick.'

His face was perfectly sober, but his eyes were laughing into hers. She fought to hold on to her anger. 'You're hurting me,' she complained.

'I don't think so. I'm just making sure you don't try it again.'

She allowed her eyes to widen and her mouth to tremble pathetically. 'I promise I won't.'

'Forgive me if I don't believe you. Anyway, I rather like this position.'

There was no pretence in her sudden indrawn breath, nor in the fear that flared her nostrils. Unconsciously, she used the very word he had been looking for earlier. 'Please don't——'

'Don't what, Ashley? Don't do this?' He lowered his head and briefly, lightly, brushed her lips with his.

It could scarcely be called a kiss, for it had been over before it had begun. Yet her heart was racing in her breast and she was suddenly breathless, aware along the whole length of her body of the warmth and closeness of Michael's frame, of the tautly muscled chest pushing her against the wall, and the strong fingers clasping her elbows.

Abruptly he let go of her arms, stepping back a couple of paces. 'No pass,' he said lightly. 'For a minute I nearly forgot.'

So did I. . . . She swallowed, trying to recapture her wits. Coyly she batted her lashes at him and heard herself ask, 'Please, Mr Gault, may I go back to bed now?'

He began to laugh. 'You intrigue me, Ashley-Becky-Cynthia. You can be like a little wildcat, spitting at anyone who gets near you, all your claws out. And sometimes you look as though you're bearing the weight of the whole world on your shoulders. But then you suddenly act the fool and I sense another woman under the surface struggling to get out.'

A little girl inching along the top of the fence, scared to death and exhilarated at one and the same time...
'Psychoanalysis at three a.m., Dr Gault?' she queried.

'Part of my job, and a very important part, was the ability to sum people up—fast.'

She noticed the past tense. And although she was intensely curious, she was darned if she was going to ask what that mysterious job had been. 'So now you keep in practice with your sheep?'

'Among other things... Good night, Ashley MacCulloch. Sleep well.'

Ashley bent and picked up Victoria, who moaned querulously and sucked at her fist. Taking her time, Ashley smiled full at him and repeated with exaggerated politeness, 'Good night, Michael. Do sleep well. Perhaps you wouldn't mind putting the light out for me—providing I say please, that is?'

'My pleasure.'

As she padded up the stairs, Ashley was very conscious of the man following her only a couple of steps behind. He might have a bad knee, but he still moved with a catlike stealth—and pounced with the speed and precision of a cat, too, she thought ruefully, remembering the fracas in the kitchen. She had difficulty visualising him as a sheep farmer. Altogether too domesticated an occupation for a man like him.

Going into Victoria's room, she laid the baby in her crib, pulling a yellow woollen blanket over her. Not until she turned around did she realise she had been followed. Michael's body, too close to hers for comfort, was a dark silhouette, his face in shadow. Opening her mouth to protest, she felt his hands cup her face. His mouth was warm and sure of itself, moving against hers with the certainty that he would bring her pleasure. Then he released her. 'Just a kiss, Ashley—no pass. When I make a pass at you, you'll know the difference. Good night.'

Dumbstruck, she watched him leave the room. Down the hall a door closed. Bedsprings creaked. Then there was silence.

Alone in the darkened room Ashley lifted fingers to her mouth and rested them there. It was a kiss that had been as intimate as it had been unexpected, a kiss that had left her feeling weak and uncertain of herself. *Wanting more* ... the fingers against her mouth tightened to a fist and her eyes closed. *Never again, Ashley. Never again ...*

Victoria overslept in the morning, as a result of which Ashley did, too. So when she went downstairs carrying the child in her arms, her grandfather had a fire crackling in the stove, the oatmeal bubbling in the pot, and the tea made. Michael Gault, looking very much at home, was buttering the toast.

'Morning, Ashley,' Matthew said. 'You slept in, eh? Must have been up late last night, were you? I'll look after the little one while you have your breakfast, you've got to open up the garage in a few minutes.'

'Victoria woke in the night, Grandad—that's why I slept in,' Ashley announced, avoiding Michael's amused blue eyes as he put the toast on the table.

'Good morning, Ashley,' said Michael. He took Victoria from her arms and swung the child high in the air, laughing up at her. Waving her fat fists, Victoria gurgled with delight.

She would, Ashley thought sourly. Victoria shared her great-grandfather's indiscriminate enthusiasm for the human race, and was now favouring Michael with a wide—and still toothless—grin. Ignoring both of them,

Ashley helped herself to porridge, adding generous amounts of brown sugar and thick cream. Unfortunately neither Michael nor Victoria seemed to realise they were being ignored; they were too busy making eyes at each other. *You're a bad-tempered bitch, Ashley MacCulloch. Smile! The sun's shining.*

And so it was. Through the window she could see a perfect mid-October day, the sky as blue as a day in August. Raindrops sparkled in the grass. Like a motley yet undefeated army the maples flaunted their tattered scarlet foliage; amidst the dour evergreens, the silver branches of the birches lifted a shimmering shower of gold leaves to the heavens. The beech trees, humbler, were clad in sober rusts and browns. A late robin hopped along one of the trenches in the garden, head cocked as it listened for the subterranean rustling of the worms.

Ashley was just starting her toast when a little bell rang in the back porch, the signal that someone wanted gas. She pushed back from the table. 'Won't be a minute.'

Grabbing the keys from the hook, she unlatched the back door and stepped outside, taking a deep breath of the clean morning air. It smelled of wet, fallen leaves and woodsmoke, infinitely preferable to the gasoline fumes and grease that she inhaled all day.

As she ran lightly across the grass in her jeans and T-shirt, she realised that she was glad to escape from the kitchen. She had never met a man as capable of throwing her off balance as Michael Gault; she was not sure she liked the sensation. It would be as well when he went on his way. Quickly she unlocked the office door and turned on the pumps, then ran back outside.

A truck was drawn up by the gas pumps, a new Ford half-ton with four-wheel drive. Absently admiring it, it took her a moment to realise who the driver was. Without enthusiasm she said, 'Hello, Willie. Fill it up?'

'Yeah. Unleaded.'

The man in the cab opened the door and got out. His

name was Willie Budgeon, an inappropriately harmless name, Ashley often thought. Even a slightly comical name. However, there was nothing either harmless or funny about Willie Budgeon. He was perhaps four or five years older than her twenty-two and was already foreman of a lumber crew, an achievement which meant he was ambitious, physically strong, and good with his fists: three attributes that in themselves had nothing wrong with them. Unfortunately Willie also had a mean streak in him, sometimes under control when he was sober, never when he was drinking.

Had she realised Willie was the owner of the new red truck, she would have taken the time to pull on her overalls, Ashley thought uneasily, feeling his eyes on her figure in the tight-fitting jeans and trim shirt. She inserted the nozzle in the tank and flipped it on, saying distantly, 'Nice truck. Do you need the oil checked?'

He shook his head. 'You could clean the windshield, though.'

She got the pail out of the office, flicked the excess fluid from the sponge cleaner and went up to the hood of the truck. As she stood on her toes and stretched to reach the centre of the windshield, Willie came up behind her. He rested one hand on the fender on either side of her hips.

Ashley stopped what she was doing. 'Don't, Willie.' He had tried to touch her before, but she had always managed to evade him.

'You should wear jeans all the time. You look a helluva lot better in them than you do in overalls.'

That he should be echoing Michael's sentiments the night before only made her angrier. She twisted to face him. 'I want to do the other side of the windshield. Will you move, please?'

His eyes were peculiarly light, while his hair, jet black, was slicked to his skull. His clothes were black, too, leather jacket, shirt, pants, and boots. He wore a copper bracelet around one wrist, and an assortment of medallions on chains around his neck. That two of them were religious medals did not impress Ashley, for she had concluded months ago that the distinction between good and evil had never registered in Willie's brain.

He moved one hand, but only to grab her breast and squeeze it with bruising strength. She gasped in mingled pain and outrage, slashing out at him with the windshield cleaner. Somewhat to her surprise he immediately let go of her and stepped back.

Then she followed the direction of his gaze and saw what he had seen: Michael, coming across the grass towards them. His limp was not as noticeable when he walked as when he ran. He was taller than Willie, and in his own way looked just as dangerous. He said softly, 'Having trouble, Ashley?'

Before she could answer, Willie sneered, 'Got yourself a boy-friend, eh, Ashley?' He addressed his second question to Michael; it concerned her sexual prowess, and was so crudely phrased that she flushed scarlet.

In a blur of movement Michael's fist lashed out. As Willie lurched backwards against the side of the truck, a trickle of blood appeared at the corner of his mouth. Into the silence Michael said flatly, his very lack of emphasis lending credence to his words, 'Don't you ever lay a hand on her again. Do you hear me?'

Willie straightened, wiping his mouth with the back of his hand so that the blood smeared his chin. 'I hear you, big boy,' he grated. 'Now let me tell you something. You better stay out of this town. Because if you don't, I'll get you. And you'll be staying here for good!'

His words were banal, a quote from a dozen third-grade movies. But there was nothing banal about the venom in the pale eyes. Michael, however, looked singularly unimpressed. 'I'll do what I please,' he said levelly. 'Now pay the lady for the gas and get moving.'

Carefully avoiding Willie, her hand shaking, Ashley took the nozzle and brought the total amount on the dial to an even thirty dollars. Willie tossed a couple of bills at her, got in the truck and slammed the door. The engine roared into life. His tires shooting out gravel, he swung on to the highway, not bothering to look either way to see if anything was coming.

'If he drives like that, he'll be the one who stays here for good,' remarked Michael. 'I would presume he's one of the reasons you're not enthused by the male of the species, Ashley?'

Because her hands were still trembling, it took her a minute to latch the nozzle back on the pump. 'I don't understand you!' she burst out. 'You hit him hard enough to have knocked him over if the truck hadn't been there. And now you're as cool and collected as if nothing happened. Who *are* you, Michael?'

'I told you, I'm a sheep farmer from Starr River . I also run a home for delinquent boys.'

She fought back a hysterical laugh. 'Is that how you keep them in order—the way you hit Willie?'

'Hardly—the authorities frown on that kind of thing. Don't fuss, Ashley, I've known all kinds of men like Willie. For me they're no problem. Although for you, it's another story. Does he come around here often?'

'Whenever he needs gas. But normally I'm inside and Tommy's looking after the pumps.'

'Do you get a lot of that kind of thing?'

'Not a lot. Willie's the worst, he and his crew.'

When Michael spoke this time, she could not have argued with the seriousness of his voice. 'He's a mean character, that Willie. Be careful, won't you, Ashley? Avoid being alone with him if that's at all possible.'

Ridiculously she felt a surge of happiness that Michael should concern himself with her safety. 'I will,' she said, and smiled at him, the rare, generous smile that once she had given to David and now kept solely for Victoria and Matthew.

An indefinable emotion flared in the blue eyes. 'You know, you're a very beautiful woman.'

Ashley drew back a little and said lightly, 'And a

social pariah—what a combination! Now I'd better finish my breakfast before the next customer comes.'

For a moment she thought he was going to say something else. However, he gave himself a little shake and in silence followed her back to the house.

Ashley was kept busy all morning running back and forth to the gas pumps as well as coping with some routine mechanical work: flat tires, wheel balancing, a safety inspection. She snatched a hurried sandwich at lunchtime. When the big blue and white Acadian bus pulled into the yard, she signed for the part from the Mercedes dealer. Then she got to work on Michael's car, checking her procedure first in the service manual, a book she privately called her Bible. She was finished in half an hour. After backing the car out of the garage, she checked the air pressure in all four tires; as she had suspected, the front left tire was down by several pounds.

She was looping the rubber hose back on the pressure gauge when she saw Michael leave the house and walk towards the garage. She had scarcely seen him since the episode with Willie; he had made no attempt to come to the garage and keep her company during the morning, something she had privately thought—and hoped?—he might do. And now that the Mercedes was roadworthy again, he would be gone. As he got within earshot, she said crisply, 'I'm going to take it for a road test. Would you mind asking Grandad to keep an eye on the pumps while I'm gone? I'll only be ten minutes.'

'Okay,' he drawled. 'Hopefully all kinds of people will want gas, and I'll get to look after your delightful daughter.'

Ashley pursed her lips. 'For someone who's never married, you seem very enamoured of babies.'

'I suppose so.' He paused, as if weighing his words. 'I've seen rather more than most people what terrible things human beings can do to other human beings. So when I look at Victoria I see simplicity, innocence, and trust. Because all she knows or has ever known is love. . . . I'm not so naïve as to think that it's possible or even desirable for that state of affairs to continue—she has to live in the real world and her innocence will disappear. But at the moment I'm simply enjoying her as she is. You're very lucky, Ashley.'

Ashley stood still, her eyes brilliant with unshed tears. From the moment the child had been born she had loved Victoria with an uncomplicated, even instinctive love. She would kill to protect Victoria, she knew that in her bones. But she had also been very aware that Victoria was illegitimate; that she, Ashley, had not provided the child with a father nor herself with a husband, and sometimes this awareness got in the way of the love, colouring it with pain and guilt. Now, in a few words, Michael had pointed out what a privilege it was to be Victoria's mother, an enviable privilege. According to Michael she should be grateful, not ashamed.

'I *am* lucky,' she said in a low voice. 'You're right.' She blinked furiously. 'Oh damn, it's nothing to cry about.' Rubbing at her eyes with her fists, she inadvertently left a smear of grease on her cheek. A glint of laughter appeared in Michael's eyes. Ashley could see it without being able to guess its cause; assuming he was laughing at her display of emotion, she said crossly, 'I'm going to test-drive the car. Then you can leave.'

Although she was very conscious of his eyes on her as she backed away from him, the sheer pleasure of driving a Mercedes soon superseded all other concerns. She could have been sitting in an armchair at home, so smoothly and quietly did the car run. Certainly she had solved the problem that had brought Michael Gault into her life. He could go back to his sheep farm now and his rich female friend with the elegant gloves and the gorgeous car: a conclusion which brought Ashley no joy. She accelerated going up a hill, automatically listening to the quiet purr of the motor, yet feeling none of the satisfaction she usually associated with a job well done.

Michael was still standing by the gas pumps when she drove back into the yard. She climbed out, taking with her the vinyl cover that she always used to prevent the grease from her overalls getting on the seat, and said briefly, 'You're all set. I'll make up the bill.'

He followed her into the office and stood watching as she totalled her time and the cost of parts. Taking the finished bill from her, he scanned it briefly and pulled a cheque book from his back pocket. His handwriting with its strong angular strokes was undeniably masculine and almost totally illegible. As she looked at it doubtfully, he said, 'It's all right—it won't bounce.'

'It was your handwriting I was questioning, not your credit,' she snapped, slamming the keys down on the counter. 'Goodbye.'

'Goodbye, Becky-Cynthia.'

'My name is Ashley,' she said between gritted teeth, a tiny part of her brain wondering why she should be so angry.

'A sigh in the wind . . . no, it doesn't fit.' He raised a hand in salute, and she had time to think that his eyes were like a distillation of all the blue in the sky, before he turned on his heel and walked out. Without a backward look he got in the Mercedes and drove away.

Standing very still, Ashley watched until the car was out of sight. He had made no mention of seeing her again, she thought, nor had he mouthed any of the platitudes about being happy to have met her. She had been a passing episode to him, an interesting little experience that he would soon forget. She found herself hoping he would not tell the owner of the Mercedes about the sharp-tongued and abrasive blonde who, of all things, was a mechanic with an illegitimate baby. To think of the two of them laughing at her filled her with a helpless fury and an equally strong urge to put her head down and cry.

Perhaps fortunately the bell rang, signifying a customer at the pumps. Ashley composed her face into something approaching a smile, and went outside.

CHAPTER THREE

As the pleasant October days passed, Ashley did her best to forget Michael and his brief intrusion into her life. It was surprisingly difficult to do so. For one thing her grandfather had been mightily taken with Michael, and insisted on repeating in irksome detail every scrap of conversation that had passed between the two men. He showed, moreover, a highly improper degree of curiosity into Ashley's dealings with Michael, a curiosity which in the end drove Ashley to cry, 'Grandad, I don't know why he's never married—I didn't ask him! I wish you'd drop the subject of Michael Gault. I'm heartily bored with it.'

Her cheeks were pink and her eyes stormy; she looked furious rather than bored. Matthew said shrewdly, 'You're mad as hops because you haven't heard from him since he left here.'

'I am not!'

''S funny I'd have sworn he was interested in you.'

'He was interested in me the way an entomologist is interested in the beetle that's wiggling on the pin. I was a peculiar specimen of womanhood, that's all. Now, can we change the subject?'

'Sure, sure . . . I didn't mean to upset you.'

'I'm not upset!' she said with patent untruth.

Matthew peered at her from under his shaggy brows. 'Of course you're not,' he said soothingly. 'By the way, something interesting happened this afternoon—I had a visit from Wayne McEvoy.'

'Oh? What did he want?' Wayne McEvoy was Lower Hampton's example of the local boy who had made good. As Wayne was fond of telling people, he'd been born in a tarpaper shack down by the river; he now lived in a massive mock-Tudor mansion in the nearest town, ten miles to the north of Lower Hampton, this mansion being adorned by an equally high-priced wife. He had a monopoly on the lumbering business for miles around, owned a chain of grocery stores, and was reported to be a slum landlord in Halifax. His reputation was far from spotless. Clever was a charitable word to describe him; unscrupulous was probably closer to the mark. That he should take the time to visit humble Matthew Stewart did not seem in character.

'You'd never guess in a hundred years. He wants to buy the gas station.'

'Oh ... why?' Ashley asked baldly, trying to still the panic racing along her nerves.

'Guess he's getting bored with grocery stores. Wants to branch out. I told him no deal, of course.'

Ashley let out her breath in a tiny sigh. 'Of course?' she repeated warily.

'Even though I don't put in near the hours I used to since you came along, I'd still be lost without the place. I've owned the gas station for nigh on forty years. Sell it to the likes of Wayne McEvoy? Not likely!'

'You're sure, Grandad?' Ashley said slowly. 'You're not just saying that because you know I need the work?'

'Course not, lass.' Matthew turned away, his voice gruff as it always was when he talked about his dead wife. 'I brought Bella to this house thirty-nine years ago. She helped me make the first payments on the garage, helped me build it up to the way it is today. She always had faith in it, did Bella.'

'It was you she had faith in, Grandad.'

Matthew blew his nose on a bright red handkerchief. 'Reckon you're right. Anyway, you see why I couldn't sell it—specially to Wayne McEvoy. I remember him when he was just a young fellow, nine or ten. He used to organise the other boys to pick on the little kids in the school playground. Then when the teacher came out, Wayne was always somewhere else, looking innocent as a newborn babe.'

Ridiculous that her grandfather's casually chosen

phrase should have reminded her of Michael Gault; innocent was one of the words Michael had used to describe Victoria. Wincing away from the memory, Ashley said brightly, 'Is supper nearly ready? Or do I have the time to bath Victoria first?' And the discussion about Wayne McEvoy was dropped.

But Ashley was to be reminded of it the following day. Business was slack, so she had walked the mile and a half to the post office to get the mail. Sorting through the various envelopes, most of which seemed to be bills, she heard a man's voice say, 'Hi, Ashley. Just the person I wanted to see.'

It was Wayne McEvoy. He was wearing dark glasses and a belted trench coat with a great many buttons and flaps; unkindly Ashley decided he was trying to look like a member of the Secret Service. 'Hello,' she said.

He smoothed back his suspiciously dark hair. 'Do you have a moment?'

'I should get back——'

'I promise I won't take long.' He gave her a smile that reeked of sincerity. 'Why don't we sit in my car? We can talk more comfortably there.'

His car was a custom-built navy-blue Lincoln Continental. Perversely pleased that she was in working clothes, Ashley settled herself in the passenger seat and decided to go on the offensive. 'I hear you were talking to Grandad about buying the garage,' she said, folding her hands in her lap.

'I wondered if he'd mention it to you,' Wayne said heartily. 'Yes, I'm very interested in acquiring it. Very interested.' There was a significant pause.

When it had gone on long enough, Ashley responded calmly, 'But he doesn't want to sell.'

'So he said.' Wayne gave a jovial chuckle. 'But that's where you come in.' Ashley delicately raised her eyebrows, inwardly noting how the ruthless hazel eyes did not tally with the chuckle.

'I'm hoping you can persuade him to change his mind, Ashley.'

'I don't think he'll do that, Mr McEvoy. Grandad's very attached to the whole property, he's lived there for years.'

'I'm sure you wouldn't want a little sentiment to get in the way of a good business deal, my dear. Your grandfather could come out of this very well. Very well indeed.' Wayne pulled a gold case out of his pocket and lit a cigar with a matching gold lighter.

Look impressed, Ashley. That cigar case would keep you and Victoria for several weeks. 'My grandfather's been making his own decisions all his life. He's unlikely to change now.'

For a moment Wayne's whole face matched the cold, feral eyes. 'I think you should do your best to make him change his mind, Ashley. For his sake and for yours.'

A cold hand squeezed her heart. 'What do you mean?'

He was all affability again. 'Nothing, my dear, nothing. But I do want that property. And I usually get what I want—one way or another.' He beamed at her, patting her hand, the diamonds on his finger twinkling coldly. 'You talk to him. Tell him he's getting too old for such responsibility. Tell him all the nice things he could do with the money. Buy a new car. Go on a cruise. The sky's the limit.'

The thought of Matthew's boundless curiosity and lack of tact confined for weeks on end on a cruise boat almost made Ashley smile. Almost. 'I'll discuss it with my grandfather again. That's all I can promise.'

'Do you best, won't you?' Wayne said softly. 'I'll be checking in a few days.'

Feeling as if she would suffocate if she didn't get a breath of fresh air, Ashley scrambled out of the car, slamming the door with unnecessary strength. What a horrible man Wayne McEvoy was, she fumed inwardly as she marched along the shoulder of the road towards the garage, for once oblivious to the tawny beauty of the autumn foliage. She passed Mrs Darby's house, not noticing how the net curtain flickered and was still, and then the general store, forgetting completely that she was supposed to get milk. In the ditch alongside the road the water gurgled. A blue jay's raucous cry echoed among the trees. As her brief spurt of temper cooled, the nuances of the conversation between her and Wayne began to resurface. There had been a threat under all that bonhommie. But why should the purchase of a small gas station in a very small village be of importance to Wayne McEvoy? And how could he put any kind of a threat into effect?

As she walked along the road past the unpretentious houses with their neatly kept gardens and their backdrop of forest she was frowning to herself. She could bring the subject up with Grandad ... but she was almost sure he wouldn't listen. Amenability to reason was not one of Matthew's traits.

However, over the next couple of days the opportunity did not seem to arise to speak to her grandfather about the sale of the garage. The weather had changed from sunshine to a steady, disheartening drizzle that was not only depressing but also caused Matthew's arthritis to flare up. Testy as a bear with a sore paw, he stomped around the house. Victoria seemed to catch his mood, whining fretfully and rubbing at her sore gums, her little face a study of woe. Ashley coped with both of them as best she could; naturally enough Wayne McEvoy was the last person on her mind.

It was a relief each morning after breakfast to escape to the garage, where the problems were more straightforward. Alternator belts could be adjusted, fuel pumps replaced, and valves ground; if only she could as simply eradicate Grandad's arthritis and give Victoria a full set of teeth, Ashley thought as she unscrewed the air breather in Mr Darby's old Pontiac, peering at the filters. She checked the PC valve and gave the fan-belt a half-turn. Everything okay so far. Mr Darby was as fussy about his car as his wife was about her house and her neighbour's morals. Emma Darby did not approve of Victoria.

She undid the red plastic caps on the battery; the water level was a little low. Behind her a voice said casually, 'Hello, Becky-Cynthia.'

Her heart thumped and she dropped two of the caps. They bounced off the radiator hose and fell to the floor of the pit. Turning around, Ashley said slowly, 'You do make a habit of creeping up on me, Michael Gault.'

He grinned at her. He was wearing exactly the same clothes as the last time, she thought irrelevantly, and his eyes were just as blue as she remembered them. 'Only twice,' he reproved. 'Scarcely a habit.'

'What's wrong with the Mercedes this time?' she asked sarcastically.

'I gave it back—once was enough. I've got my jeep with me.'

Through the glass panels in the door she saw a disreputable mud-stained vehicle parked on the tarmac. It had once been painted green; its cab appeared to be held together by fencing wire. 'Oh . . . that's yours?'

'All mine. It's a mechanic's dream—you should be itching to get your fingers on it.'

'Or a wrecking hammer,' she said cruelly.

'Be nice to me, Ashley . . . What are you doing?'

'An oil change and grease job.'

'How long will you be?'

'Ten more minutes.'

'Then what?'

'Nothing at the moment.'

'Good.' He bestowed another smile on her, which to her annoyance made her heart engage in further peculiar antics. 'We'll take Victoria for a walk. I'm in love with Victoria.'

'Victoria's sleeping.'

'No, she's not. I checked—she's yelling her head off.'

'Oh, no!' groaned Ashley.

'You finish here,' Michael said kindly. 'I'll go and get her dressed, that'll cheer her up.'

'It's raining.'

'It's stopped.'

She glared at him. 'Give me one good reason why I should go for a walk with you.'

'Because, appearances to the contrary, you're pleased to see me, aren't you, Ashley? By the way, don't forget to pick up those little red things.'

Before she could think of a suitably cutting retort he was gone. She stamped her steel-toed boot on the cement floor as hard as she could, a childish action that nevertheless made her feel better. Then, as he had suggested, she climbed down the narrow steps into the pit and picked up the battery caps from the sawdust-covered floor.

It was nearly twenty minutes before she drove Mr Darby's car outside and parked it under the trees, for she had had to replace a couple of fuses and pump up the spare tire. Telling Tommy that she was going to the house, she walked across the grass. Michael was right; it had stopped raining. A capricious wind shook the raindrops from the sodden boughs of the spruce trees and tugged the vivid leaves from the maples, while grey-edged clouds scudded across the sky. Yet some of the warmth of summer still lingered in the air.

In the back porch she pulled off her work clothes. Victoria was no longer yelling; instead, through the closed door that led into the kitchen, Ashley could hear gurgles of delight. It came as no surprise, therefore, to find Michael dandling the child on his knee as he drank a cup of Matthew's horrendously strong coffee. She said in exasperation, 'You'll be the ruination of that child!'

'Ready to go?'

'Where on earth will we go?'

'For a walk. It'll do you good.'

So he wanted a walk, did he? She said grimly, 'Give me a minute to change, okay?'

Upstairs, she took off her work clothes and pulled on her tightest jeans and a bright red sweater that hugged her breasts. She bundled her hair high on her head, topped it with a scarlet beret and applied a liberal coating of cherry-red lipstick. Her bomber jacket and Frye boots completed the picture. Swaggering a little in front of the mirror, she decided they'd go to the store, the post office and the bank: that should cure Michael's urge for a walk. The heels of her boots clattering on the stairs, she went back into the kitchen, swinging her hips.

Matthew was getting wood from the basement. For her ears alone Michael murmured, 'The scarlet woman of Lower Hampton.'

Not at all surprised that he had caught the allusion, Ashley fluttered her mascaraed lashes. 'Exactly. You still want to go?'

'I wouldn't miss it for anything.'

She picked up her handbag from the table. 'I have a few errands to do. Victoria's carriage is in the back porch.' She called goodbye to her grandfather and preceded Michael outdoors. He propped Victoria up in the carriage. 'I'll wheel her,' he said.

Better and better, thought Ashley mischievously, feeling as if the little girl who had loved to play rowdy games with her brothers had been liberated again. Sedately they proceeded down the road.

The first stop was the general store, which sold everything from finishing nails to ground steak. Michael picked Victoria up and they went inside. Emma Darby was standing in front of a rack of housedresses that was squeezed between some galvanised pails and a display of highly coloured birthday cards; she saw them immediately. Her pale blue eyes bulging out of her head with curiosity, she sniffed, 'Good morning, Miss MacCulloch.' She always called Ashley Miss MacCulloch. She was president of the local gardening club and the laidies' aid, neither of which groups Ashley had been invited to join.

'Good morning, Mrs Darby,' Ashley said clearly. 'May I introduce a friend of mine, Michael Gault? Victoria, of course, you know.'

Mrs Darby inclined her head graciously. 'I don't

believe I've seen you before, Mr Gault. Are you from around here?'

'No, I'm not, Mrs Darby, I'm from Starr River. But I expect you'll be seeing more of me in the future. You'll excuse us, won't you? We have rather a lot to do. What do you need here, Ashley?'

'Bread and milk,' Ashley said faintly; she had never been able to snub Mrs Darby quite so effectively.

From the general store they went to the post office, where Michael collected more than his share of curious stares, and from there to the bank. After conducting her business, Ashley rejoined Michael in the lobby. As she did so, a man pushed open the door. It was Wayne McEvoy, in an expensively tailored wool overcoat that contrived to look as if the wrong man was wearing it. 'Why, Ashley,' he said cordially, ignoring Michael after one quick glance in his direction. 'I've been meaning to give you a call about the little matter we discussed the other day.'

'I haven't done anything about it,' she said flatly.

'I see . . . but I'm sure you'll remedy that, won't you? Why don't I get in touch with you at the first of the week? And now aren't you going to introduce your friend?'

Ashley mumbled the introductions. There was no logical reason why she should feel afraid; if the garage wasn't for sale, it wasn't for sale, and Wayne would simply have to accept that. But her heart was racing and her throat felt tight, and she had to conquer an absurd impulse to grab Victoria from Michael and hold the child as closely as she could.

After Wayne had said goodbye, she, Michael, and Victoria went out into the playful wind. Ashley said abruptly, 'Let's go home.'

'What's wrong?'

'I don't like him, that's all.'

'Not a man to trust, I wouldn't think.'

Ashley was spared the necessity of replying as they passed three ladies from the local church group, all of whom nodded at Ashley and gaped at Michael. The sense of adventure which had prompted Ashley to put on the red sweater and hat had vanished. She said peevishly, 'It'll be all over the village by tonight that Ashley MacCulloch's got herself a new man—you realise that, don't you?'

'I can stand it.'

'They'll say we're sleeping together.'

'We know we're not.'

'Doesn't *anything* ever bother you?' she exploded.

'Of course,' he said shortly. 'But not gossip, that's all.'

'It's all right for you, you don't have to live here.'

'You're really spoiling for a fight, aren't you?'

'So why don't you oblige?' she demanded shrewishly.

'All right, I will.' His eyes were brilliant with an answering anger. 'You've got a chip on your shoulder the size of a barn.'

'What the hell do you mean?'

'I'm referring to Victoria. Sure, some of the older people around here have difficulty with an unmarried mother, that's the way they were brought up. But I bet you don't go out of your way to change them or to look for the people who might think differently. You'd rather wear a hair shirt. Ashley MacCulloch, mother of an illegitimate child. Stay away.'

Deep inside Ashley knew there might be more than a grain of truth in his words, which only served to make her angrier. 'I *am* an unmarried mother!' she choked.

'Why wouldn't he marry you, Ashley?'

Michael's voice was very quiet; his question stopped her dead in her tracks, dissipating her anger. She shoved her hands in the pockets of her bomber jacket. 'I could give you all kinds of reasons,' she said in a dull voice. 'But I suppose essentially it was because he didn't love me enough.'

'Who is he? How did you meet him?'

She stared past her companion into the gold and green of the woods, dimly aware of the rustle of the leaves and the sighing of the wind in the spruce boughs as she pictured David in her mind's eye. His dark hair had always been tousled, his smile charming. But somehow the exact colour of his eyes and the shape of his mouth now eluded her. 'His name is David Ainsley,' she said. 'He was a second-year medical student at the University of Western Ontario when I met him, so quite a bit older than me. I was in my first year of engineering; I'd already taken the mechanics course.' She shrugged. 'What is there to say? We met in January, we dated all spring, we fell in love. And in the summer we—made love. It just happened. It wasn't planned. I—I'd never intended to . . .' Her voice died away.

'Give yourself a break, Ashley,' Michael said roughly. 'You were young and in love. It's a perfectly natural progression of events.'

'I was brought up to think it was wrong. But I *loved* him!'

'So then what?'

'When I found out I was pregnant, David was horrified. He had three more years of medical school, a year of internship, and then he wanted to specialise. He couldn't afford to saddle himself with a wife and child—those were his precise words. When I refused to have an abortion, he stopped seeing me. He's never seen Victoria.'

The cause of the discussion gave an indignant squawk from the carriage, for Victoria preferred motion to being stationary. Starting to wheel the carriage again, Michael said, 'Then he's the loser, isn't he?'

'Oh, I suppose so,' sighed Ashley. 'Maybe all men are like that—taking their fun and then leaving when the going gets rough.'

'Not all of them, Ashley.'

'How do you know?' she flared. 'What about you? You've never married. But I'd be willing to bet you haven't lived a celibate life.'

'If I haven't, then I have never deluded my partner with promises of undying love,' he retorted. 'The cards were always on the table. We both understood what was—and was not—involved.'

'How very sophisticated,' she said in a brittle voice. 'You must think I'm an awful fool.'

'I think you were young and trusting and in love.'

'I did trust him.' She looked up; she had never expressed this to anyone before. 'And I loved him. But now I'm not sure if he really did love me or if he just said so because he wanted my body.'

'Does it really matter? You loved him, you know that. You can only take responsibility for your own feelings, Ashley, not for his as well.'

'Oh—you mean because I loved him I was acting in good faith?' It was a novel point of view, one she wanted to think about. She said unnecessarily, 'We're nearly home.'

'So we are.' Michael's steps slowed. 'A moment ago you said you loved him. Past tense. Is it in the past, Ashley?'

'When David told me to destroy the child we'd created, he destroyed the love I'd felt for him, too. It was as if scales fell off my eyes, as if I'd been blind . . . I don't think I'll ever dare fall in love again in case the same thing happened.'

'It wasn't the quality of your love that was at fault. It was the man you chose to bestow it on.'

Because the shoulder of the road was narrow, she was standing very close to Michael. 'I don't know why I'm telling you all this,' she whispered. 'I don't usually talk about it.'

'You're starting to trust me, Ashley.'

She visibly recoiled. 'No! I just finished saying I wouldn't trust a man again. Not ever.'

'Never is a very long time.' He grinned crookedly. 'We'll have to continue this discussion another day—I've got to leave, I have some business in Halifax this afternoon. Are you free on Saturday night? I thought we might go into the city together. We could have dinner and go to the theatre.'

Ashley gaped at him. 'Me?'

'You've got it wrong again, Ashley. You're supposed to say, *Thank you, Michael, I'd be delighted to go with you.*'

'I'm out of practice,' she said drily. 'Why me, Michael?'

'How about because I like you?'

'No, you don't. You think I'm a bitchy female with a chip on her shoulder.'

'I also think you're brave and hard-working and very loving.'

'Oh.' She blushed, her grey eyes suddenly vulnerable.

'And under that somewhat inhibited exterior I'm convinced there's a woman who enjoys taking risks and having fun. I'd like to see more of that woman ... Besides which, talking of seeing more of you, I'd like to see you in a dress.'

She blushed more deeply, her cheeks the same colour as her sweater, and blurted, 'I—I'm not out for a good time, Michael.'

'Let's not use euphemisms, Ashley,' he said harshly. 'You think I'm asking you out because I want to take you to bed? I'm a normal male, and you're a particularly attractive female who happens to be poured into that outfit you're wearing. But that's not why I'm asking you out. No funny business. Anyway, no matter what the circumstances, I'd never force you to do anything you didn't want to do.'

'I wanted to the last time—with David,' she muttered.

'Then next time you'll be more cautious, won't you? So what's the answer—yes or no?'

It was the old lure of the balancing act on the fence high above the ground. 'Yes, I'll go,' she said rashly.

'Good. I'll pick you up a little after six. We'll probably eat after the theatre, otherwise it's a bit of a rush.'

They had reached the jeep. 'Will I get to drive in that?' Ashley queried dubiously.

'I do have a car that I drag out for ceremonial occasions. Also a suit.'

'We'll hardly recognise each other.'

He reached out a hand and stroked a strand of hair back from her face. 'Oh, yes, we will—I'd recognise your hair anywhere,' he said, a husky note in his voice.

She saw how his eyes darkened and felt the warmth of his fingers brush her cheek. Her heart fluttered in her breast with the first tentative stirring of desire. And then, with the speed of a striking snake, panic clamped a stranglehold on desire. She had felt desire before and had lived with the consequences, both physical and emotional, ever since. She stepped back, grabbing the handle of the carriage and saying breathlessly, 'I've got to go.'

'Until Saturday.' Closing the gap between them, Michael kissed her firmly on the lips, turned on his heel and got in the jeep. A casual wave of his hand and an outraged roar from the jeep, and he was driving away.

What does he want of me? she wondered, absently rocking the carriage back and forth, in her nostrils the stink of the jeep's exhaust fumes. And what did she really know about him? Factually, very little. Yet already she recognised in him tolerance coexisting with intensity, and intelligence embellished by emotional sensitivity. He had seen beyond her guilt and confusion to the love she had for Victoria; for him that was of supreme importance. The rest scarcely mattered.

She trundled the carriage past the gas pumps, knowing he had also been right about her attitude to the people of Lower Hampton. She had arrived here last year feeling as though Unmarried Mother was written in capital letters on her forehead, and naturally she had found the Mrs Darbys and the Willie Budgeons, for they exist everywhere. But others in the village had been willing to accept her as she was, and it was these people she had been in danger of ignoring.

She was very thoughtful for the rest of the day, parrying her grandfather's inevitable questions absentmindedly. She had to tell him about her date on Saturday night because he would be staying home with Victoria; she was too preoccupied to notice that his only comment was a long-drawn out, 'Well now ... would you believe it?' As the day approached, she grew more preoccupied rather than less, and by six o'clock on Saturday evening was in a fine state of nerves that was only slightly lessened by a naïve pleasure in her own appearance.

It was literally months since she had been out on a date; certainly she had not had the opportunity to dress up since Victoria was born. So it was an unaccustomed Ashley whom she saw in the full-length mirror in the bathroom, a slender, glowing creature with wide, excited eyes. She was wearing a full-skirted chiffon dress with ruffles at the wrist and more ruffles hiding the plunge of the neckline; the fabric was a misty blend of mauve, grey, and pale blue. Her hair was fastened with a silver clip so that it fell straight down her back, shimmering under the light.

As she was putting on tiny silver earrings, Ashley heard conversation from downstairs, and knew Michael had arrived. Feeling like a teenager on her first date rather than a twenty-two-year-old who had a child of her own, she counted to ten very slowly and started down the stairs. As she pushed open the door into the kitchen, Michael turned to face her, and for a moment they looked at each other in silence.

He was the same man, yet subtly different. His eyes were as blue as they had ever been, his shoulders as broad, his unconscious air of confidence as much a part of him as his height. Yet his charcoal-grey suit, which fitted him to perfection, imparted to him an urbanity, a sophistication that somehow frightened her, for it seemed to remove him from her ken, to speak of a world that was not her world. 'Hello, Michael,' she said nervously.

Disregarding Matthew's presence Michael came closer, rested his hands on her shoulders and kissed her, first on one cheek, then on the other. 'Don't want to ruin your lipstick,' he said with mock gravity.

'You look very nice,' she offered, knowing even as she spoke that nice was totally the wrong word to describe his disturbing aura of masculinity. He looked heart-stoppingly attractive, if the truth were told, she thought fuzzily. For the first time she allowed herself to compare him with David, and recognised how much more strength and character there was in Michael's face.

'And you look very beautiful.' He looked over his shoulder. 'Doesn't she, Matthew?'

For once Matthew was bereft of speech. He was tamping tobacco into his pipe with great vigour, his shaggy brows hiding his expression. But Ashley knew him well. In quick distress she asked, 'What's the matter, Grandad?'

Still staring into the bowl of his pipe, Matthew growled, 'For a minute there you reminded me of my Bella when she was young. She got all dressed up one evening, we were going to a wedding. You look like her, that's all.' He spilt some tobacco and muttered something under his breath.

'That's a lovely compliment, Grandad.' She left Michael's hold and dropped a kiss on his bent head. 'Thank you.'

'Off you go, now,' he grunted. 'Enjoy yourselves.'

And they did. As she settled herself in the passenger seat of Michael's undistinguished Chevrolet, Ashley felt shy at first. But Michael drew her out about her grandfather and the history of the little village, so that they were talking animatedly by the time they reached the harbour city of Halifax with its twin gold-lit bridges and its destroyers anchored in the dockyard. The theatre was crowded with well-dressed people; Ashley couldn't help noticing how she and Michael attracted several second glances, and her confidence increased, as did her pride in her escort. The play, which was Tom Stoppard's *Rosencrantz and Guildenstern Are Dead*, addressed the horrific absurdities of life and the certainty of death, and was witty, thought-provoking, and disturbing.

Afterwards she and Michael walked arm in arm down the sloped streets towards the water where the tugboats were moored and the lighthouse winked on George's Island, once the site of a prison. The restaurant was in an old stone building that had been a brewery, its mahogany panelling part of the former boardroom. Green-shaded lamps cast a soft glow on the diners. A fire flickered in the brick hearth.

Influenced partly by the play, partly by the alcohol she was drinking, Ashley found herself telling Michael about her family. She described her favourite brother Bob and the episode of the fence; she attempted to put into words the constrictions of her childhood and youth. 'My father was very strict, far more so with me than with the boys. I was a mere girl, after all,' she said cynically. 'My mother was completely subjugated by him. I think she was frightened of him—hard to believe that of a daughter of Matthew's, isn't it? I was frightened of him, too, although I tried never to show it . . . There wasn't much joy in that house. No kissing or hugging, not much laughter. Life was a serious business of rules to be obeyed and moral standards to be adhered to . . . although I never really understood why. None of it seemed to be dictated by love.' Her grey eyes were faraway. 'There was a battle royal when I applied for the mechanics course. *Think of all the men you'd be associating with* . . . you'd be surprised with how much horror my mother could say the word "men". But my brothers all backed me up and in the end I went. There was only a very minor fight when I enrolled in engineering, which is ironic when you think about it, because that's when I got in trouble.'

'It sounds like a classic case of a young girl reaching out for the warmth and tenderness she never got from her father.'

Ashley shrugged, running her fingers down the stem of her wine glass. 'Maybe so.' Certainly David had radically altered her life. Like the hero of romantic fiction, he had been handsome, clever, and sophisticated. She had been bowled over when he sought her out for attention, dazzled when he courted her, and far too naïve to anticipate his physical ardour, or to resist it.

She picked up the thread of her narrative. 'My parents disowned me when I got pregnant. How old-fashioned that sounds! Like David, my father wanted me to have an abortion, while my mother went around wringing her hands and weeping about the disgrace I'd brought on them all. Talk about Victorian melodrama! Except, of course, that it was real. I was quite literally turned out of the house.' She shivered, seeing not the jewel-red of the wine but her father's face, thin-lipped, self-righteous, grey eyes like stone.

'What did you do?'

Her lashes flickered up. 'Why do you look so angry?'

'I've never been able to tolerate that narrow kind of morality that denies our very human striving for intimacy and love,' Michael said roughly. 'I'm also beginning to understand a little better the origin of the chip on your shoulder.'

'I really felt as if I'd done a terrible wrong and that I was being punished for it. That was the way my father's world worked. But when Victoria was born, and she was so beautiful and so lovable, his code seemed less applicable; certainly less powerful—' she toyed with her fork, ending in a rush '—when you told me how lucky I was to have her,' she retreated still further, 'I . . . you're quite right—I am lucky. And while I may have been wrong to have slept with David, I did it out of love, however misguided.'

Michael covered her hand with hers. 'I'm glad you understand that, Ashley.'

The tenderness in his eyes made her tremble inwardly, while the touch of his hand seemed to enfold her whole body in warmth and a deep, unreasoning happiness. For a moment that happiness shone in her eyes, clear and unguarded.

Without hurry Michael removed his hand and picked up his glass. 'To the new Ashley,' he said gently, and drank deep of the wine. Then he skilfully guided the conversation into lighter channels.

In Ashley's memory that was always to remain a magical evening. When they left the restaurant they strolled along the waterfront past the ferry dock to the mooring of the schooner *Bluenose*, proud memento of Nova Scotia's sailing ships. They went into a bar and danced. They walked back to the car past Parade Square where long ago had marched platoons of redcoats. They drove home through the star-spangled October night, and eventually Ashley's eyes drooped shut and her head fell on Michael's shoulder, her hair streaming down his sleeve. She was deeply asleep when he pulled up by her grandfather's house. The back door light was on; the rest of the house was in darkness.

'Wake up, Ashley. We're home!'

His voice seemed to come from a very long way away. She opened her eyes, blinking, and felt his arm go around her and his cheek rest on her hair: a state of affairs she found she did not want to alter. 'You mean we're home already?' she murmured.

'You slept the whole way.'

'Oh.' She yawned. 'It was a lovely evening, Michael— thank you. I enjoyed every minute of it.' She tilted her head so that she could see him, her mouth still soft with sleep. It seemed the most natural thing in the world that his mouth should find hers. He had kissed her before, but never like this: a deep, sensual probing that made her body spring to awareness and her heart hammer in her breast. Her lips parted. His tongue sought hers, his arms brushing her breast so that her flesh leaped in response.

Never again, Ashley . . . never again. The words came from nowhere, yet they were as clear a warning as if someone had spoken them. She stiffened, pulling back. 'Please, Michael, don't——' she said frantically.

He released her immediately. She could hear his quickened breathing, which only increased her fear. 'I'm sorry,' she faltered. 'I just——'

'But you felt it, didn't you, Ashley?' he interrupted, his voice harsh with emotion. 'For a minute you wanted me as badly as I want you.'

'Yes, I felt it,' she whispered. 'But it frightened me, Michael. Because I felt that way with David.'

All the considerable force of Michael's personality was behind his words. 'With me you don't have to be frightened.'

Could it be true? Or should she be more frightened than she had ever been in her life? For Michael was a far more formidable man than David, she knew that already; Michael would woo her not only with his body but with his emotions; he would be capable of a tenderness that in no way negated his masculinity.

She sat up straighter, pleating the flimsy chiffon of her skirt between her fingers. 'I don't know. I just don't know,' she said helplessly.

'I want to see you again. You know that, don't you?' *Why*, she wanted to cry. *Why do you want to see me again?* 'So you can make a pass at me?' she said, her voice quivering a little in spite of herself. 'You implied once that you would.'

He raked his fingers through his hair. 'So I did. And under the circumstances it was a damn fool thing to say, even in jest. I didn't know you then, Ashley, not as well as I'm starting to know you. I'm sorry I ever said it.'

How could she argue with such a straightforward apology? Yet it did nothing to allay her fears. Whether he labelled sexual desire as a pass or as a very human striving for intimacy and love, was not the result the same? An encounter that would bring her pain and discomfort, without any satisfaction and certainly without any loss of self-consciousness? The poets promised that the heavens would shake and the stars would fall. The poets were wrong.

She said hurriedly, 'You can call me if you like.' She fumbled for her handbag on the floor of the car. 'Goodbye.'

'Good night, not goodbye. Don't run away from me, Ashley. I promise I won't hurt you.'

'How can you know that?' she cried. In swift compunction she added, 'Oh, Michael, I'm sorry. I didn't mean to end such a beautiful evening on a note like this. But—don't let yourself get too involved with me, will you?' She attempted a smile. 'You'd be wasting your time.'

'You let me be the judge of that. I'll phone you, Ashley.'

She bit her lip, seeing the strong line of his jaw and the inflexibility in the dark-shadowed eyes. 'You may phone,' she said carefully. 'I may or may not answer.'

'You'll answer.' In a swift change of mood he added, 'I'll set Matthew on you if you don't.'

She was glad to laugh back. 'Don't you dare—I'd never hear the last of it!'

'Good night, Ashley.' His kiss was brief, making no demands. 'Take care of yourself.'

'You, too.' She gave him a quick smile, shut the car door as quietly as she could, and unlocked the back door. By the time she entered the house, he was heading for the highway. Her shoes in her hand, she tiptoed up the stairs.

CHAPTER FOUR

THE rule that misfortunes occur in threes did not hold true for Ashley on the Monday after her date with Michael: there were only two of them. But each in its own way was enough to darken her mood.

Tommy had gone for his lunch break, so she was working the gas pumps as well as trying to discover how water was leaking into the back seat of a flashy white Camaro. This latter problem involved not only hosing down the rear windows to see if the seal was broken but also getting down on her knees with a drop light and running water around the back wheel of the jacked-up car to check for holes. It was a messy and uncomfortable procedure. Her overalls were wet and her face dirty by the time she located the source of the trouble: a hole no bigger than a dime high up in the wheel well. She gave a grunt of satisfaction and got up to turn off the hose. As she did so, the bell rang. Someone wanted gas.

Ashley ran outside, her mind more on the patching of the hole than on the prospective customer. And then she almost tripped over the cord that activated the bell signal, because the car drawn up at the pumps was a black Mercedes, a 280S. As she came round the island, she saw that the driver was a woman. There was no one in the passenger seat.

Ashley could hear her blood drumming in her ears. As she rounded the hood of the Mercedes, the thought uppermost in her mind was that she looked her worst— hair tucked under her old khaki cap, dirty overalls, no make-up. She stopped by the driver's door and said politely, 'May I help you?'

The woman had rolled down the window. If Ashley had had any thoughts that Michael might have told the owner of the Mercedes about the blonde-haired mechanic he had met in Lower Hampton, they were instantly disabused. The face raised to hers was clear-eyed and open, incapable of any deception. It was also a very beautiful face.

With a friendly smile the woman said, 'Would you fill the tank, please? And check the oil?' She passed Ashley a credit card; she was wearing the brown gloves that had been so carelessly left on the dashboard.

The name in raised gold letters on the card was Mary L. Gibson. Her movements as stiff as the smile on her face, Ashley put the card in her breast pocket, started the pump running and once again raised the hood of the Mercedes. The oil level was down less than half a pint. In a colourless voice she relayed this information to Mary Gibson.

'Thanks—no need to worry, then. It's a beautiful day, isn't it?'

It was until you came along . . . 'Lovely,' said Ashley. 'Although we had a frost last night.'

'Did you? That's one advantage of living in Halifax, we don't get the extremes of temperature that you get inland.' Another friendly smile.

Mary Gibson's hair was a smooth cap of burnished copper, curling just below her ears, which were adorned with tiny gold studs. Her eyes, exquisitely set under dark-winged brows, were a warm chocolate-brown. She was wearing a taupe suede jacket with an ivory silk blouse; gold bracelets jingled on her wrist.

Michael must be in love with you . . . you're gorgeous. As well as friendly, confident, and rich. In a sickening attack of self-deprecation, Ashley heard her inner voice add caustically, *All the things you're not, Ashley MacCulloch. You're the argumentative blonde with the chip on your shoulder and the illegitimate baby on your hip.*

The nozzle clicked off. Ashley topped up the tank and called out the total, running to the office to fill in the credit slip. Mary Gibson signed it with a flourish. 'Thank you,' she said. 'Have a nice day.'

Clutching the red plastic clipboard she used for credit cards, Ashley watched the Mercedes leave the yard and turn right. Michael's sheep farm was in that direction. Mary Gibson must be going to visit Michael.

She trailed back into the garage, plunking herself down on a couple of used tyres and propping her chin in her hands. The leak in the Camaro no longer interested her in the slightest. The tangle of emotions located somewhere around the pit of her stomach could only be called jealousy, she thought wretchedly. She was jealous of Mary Gibson. She hated the thought of Michael spending the rest of the day—and the night?—with the beautiful red-haired woman who had smiled at her in such a friendly way. It would have been easier to bear if Mary Gibson had been haughty or arrogant or rude. But she had been as pleasant as she was beautiful . . . *oh, damn*!

Ashley's supply of profanity was not large. She went through it all and felt not one whit better. She might still have been sitting there an hour later if Tommy hadn't thudded down the steps calling, 'You can go to lunch now, Ashley . . . are you feeling okay?'

She glanced at him ruefully. 'Monday morning blues,' she said. 'Maybe food will help. I'll be back in an hour.'

She was almost through the door when the phone rang. Riveted to the spot, she watched Tommy pick up the receiver, wondering sickly what she would say if it were Michael.

'For you,' said Tommy, handing her the receiver. Whistling cheerfully, he went outdoors.

'MacCulloch's Garage,' croaked Ashley.

'Wayne McEvoy speaking, Ashley. How are you?'

'I'm fine.' She was telling a lot of lies today.

'Has your grandfather reconsidered?'

'I haven't spoken to him yet.'

A pause. 'Then I suggest you do so immediately.'

'I'm quite sure he won't change his mind.'

'Try, Ashley. Try hard. I'll call you back at four.' With a click the connection was cut.

She slammed the receiver back on the hook. Just what she needed ... Wayne McEvoy down her neck, today of all days! She tramped over to the house, stripped off her work clothes, and went into the kitchen. Victoria gave her an entrancing smile. Banging her plastic rattle on the tray of her high chair, she then flung the rattle to the floor, chortling gleefully at the noise it made.

For a moment the cares of the day disappeared. This was a newly learned game of Victoria's, one she would have played all day if only the adults would have co-operated. Ashley bent and picked up the rattle, shaking it and dancing around the high chair to the rhythm. Victoria shrieked with delight.

'What kind of a racket is this?' asked Matthew mildly, emerging from the pantry with a plate of sandwiches. 'Soup's hot, Ashley. Sit and eat.'

From unlikely combinations of ingredients that Ashley preferred not to analyse, Matthew produced mouthwatering soups. Ashley helped herself, and spooned some warmed-up baby food into Victoria's dish. 'I'm glad you have to eat that and not me,' she said to the child darkly. 'Grandad, I spoke to Wayne McEvoy one day last week, I forgot to tell you. He's wondering if you'll reconsider his offer. For some reason he's really anxious to buy the garage.'

'I told him no then and I'll tell him the same again,' Matthew grunted. Then his curiosity got the better of him. 'Did he offer more money?'

'No, I don't think so. He thought you could go on a cruise with the proceeds, though.'

Matthew snorted. 'I get sick in a rowboat on a pond. How's the soup?'

'Wonderful.'

'Do you want me to sell, Ashley?'

She spooned a mouthful of mush into Victoria's mouth, giving herself time to consider her reply. 'You know how happy I am here, Grandad. I don't know what I would have done without you the past year or so—the best thing Bob ever did was to arrange that I come here to live. But if you want to sell the garage, you mustn't stop on my account. I'm sure I could get a job somewhere else.'

She was not at all sure. And she knew she'd never find anyone who would take as good care of Victoria as Matthew did. But neither could she use her grandfather, he had been too good to her for that.

Matthew helped himself to a sandwich. 'I'm attached to this place, I told you that. Besides, I like living with you and Victoria, it's a lot better than being alone.'

'You're sure?'

'Sure I'm sure. Have a sandwich.'

For Matthew that was clearly the end of the discussion. Well, she'd done her best. Wayne McEvoy would have to buy a gas station somewhere else.

When the telephone rang sharp at four, Ashley had just finished doing a complete brake job on a Pontiac sedan, a task which had occupied all her attention. So her, 'MacCulloch's Garage,' was abstracted rather than businesslike.

'Wayne McEvoy. Will he sell?'

Wayne was no longer bothering to be polite. Ashley's chin tilted. 'I'm sorry, Mr McEvoy, he won't consider it——'

'Is he holding out for more money?'

'I don't think money is the issue.' She added flippantly, 'And cruises don't turn him on.'

'Very funny... Ashley, I don't think you quite understand. I am going to buy the garage, one way or another. I'd hoped he would be civilised and above board about it. But apparently that's not going to work. So I'll have to apply a little pressure, won't I?'

Any amusement she might have felt had vanished. She said coldly, 'I'm not sure I know what you mean.'

'There are all kinds of ways I could force you to sell. For obvious reasons I don't want to damage the physical premises or the goodwill of the garage. But I could get some of the lumbermen to pay you a little visit. And you have a small daughter, I believe . . . you wouldn't want anything to happen to her, would you? Or to your grandfather, for that matter. Why don't you discuss all this with him? I'm sure he'll agree the three of you are in a very vulnerable position.'

'That's extortion,' Ashley said blankly.

'Just a little friendly persuasion, Ashley. If you're sensible, nothing need happen.'

'I'll call the police!'

'Oh, I wouldn't do that if I were you. No witnesses, for one thing. And I could guarantee there'd be a nasty accident to at least one of you if you were to be so foolish.'

'Why do you want the garage?' demanded Ashley, trying very hard to maintain at least a vestige of control over the conversation.

'Not your concern, my dear. By the way, don't go telling any of this to your detective friend, will you?'

'My who?' she repeated stupidly.

'Michael Gault. The man I met you with the other day. I did a little checking up on him. You mean he hasn't told you about his—er—somewhat varied career?'

'I don't know what you're talking about.'

'Dear me . . . He was a policeman for at least ten years, and an undercover narcotics agent for a good part of that time. The official version is that he resigned. Actually he was fired. General incompetence, rumours of theft, plus a strong suspicion he was hooked on drugs himself.'

Ashley had a nightmare sense of unreality. *'Michael?'* she said incredulously. 'We can't be talking about the same man!'

'He's a con artist, my dear. That was his job, pretending to be someone he wasn't. You wouldn't be the first person he's fooled.'

Wayne's disparagement of Michael, rather than distressing her, had released in her a heady and reviving anger. 'Have you quite finished?' she said rudely.

'Because I have better things to do than listen to this nonsense!'

'Not a word I've said is intended as a joke, Ashley,' Wayne said malevolently. 'It looks as though I have to demonstrate that to you.'

She heard a click and then the burr of the engaged signal. Staring at the receiver as if Wayne himself might materialise from the mouthpiece with his expensive, ill-fitting clothes and ruthless eyes, she found herself wondering if the conversation had actually taken place. She, her daughter, and her grandfather were being threatened by a man not fit to tie her grandfather's boots, a small-town crook who would pay others to do his dirty work while he stayed safely in the background and reaped the profits. It was intolerable! Infuriating, crazy, ridiculous! The adjectives came tumbling from her brain. But it was also true. Wayne had not been joking. He was willing to apply coercion of the crudest—and most effective—kind to get what he wanted.

Slowly she replaced the receiver. So Michael had been a detective. Instinctively she knew it for the truth, because it explained so much. Her first impression of him that he could fade unnoticed into a crowd. His swift, silent movements and his efficient attack on Willie. His allusion to a world where murder and cruelty were the norm.

Why had he not shared all this with her? Particularly on Saturday night, when they had talked for so long.

Because you talked too much, Ashley. You burbled on about your unhappy childhood and your pregnancy and didn't give him a chance to get a word in . . .

But that was not true. There had been plenty of cues for Michael to have described his own past, had he chosen to do so. So why had he remained silent? Because he was ashamed of episodes in his career? Because—briefly she closed her eyes—he had been a drug addict?

It couldn't be true, she thought frantically. Wayne

was trying to poison her mind against Michael; and he was succeeding. She found she was pressing her palms to her face, as if by physical force she could blot out the ugly images crowding her brain. The Michael she knew was not a liar and a thief. Couldn't be.

After a while she went back into the garage and replaced the wheels of the Pontiac, tightening the bolts with a torque wrench and then releasing the air pressure on the hoist. She parked the car outside, stashed away her tools, and swept the garage floor, moving like a robot rather than a flesh-and-blood woman. When she went back to the house at supper-time, she still had not decided whether to tell Matthew about the phone call.

She thought she was behaving normally as she fed Victoria and described the difficulty she had had grinding the rotors. When the baby was settled in her playpen and she and Matthew were seated in the rocking chairs by the fire drinking their coffee, her grandfather asked with unusual diplomacy, 'Anything bothering you, Ashley? Worried you haven't heard from Michael? I'm sure you will. He's a busy man, you know.'

The episode with Mary Gibson seemed to have happened a lifetime ago. 'Oh, no,' she stammered.

'Then what is it?'

It was useless to try and avoid the issue, for Matthew had the tenacity of a bulldog when his curiosity was aroused. 'Wayne McEvoy phoned me this afternoon. He's making all kinds of threats, Grandad, if we don't sell.'

Her grandfather took a noisy gulp of his coffee. He did not look particularly surprised, she noticed. 'Tell me about them,' he invited.

So she did. By the time she had finished, only omitting the part about Michael, her grandfather was sitting up straight in his chair, his moustache bristling. 'That two-bit double-dealing crook!' he bellowed. 'So he thinks he can scare me into selling, does he? We'll see about that!'

'Grandad, he meant every word of it.'

'I remember Wayne McEvoy when he was a snivelling little brat in kindergarten. He used to like killing sparrows with his sling-shot—he always picks on something smaller, have you noticed that? If he thinks I'm going to turn over this place as meekly as a newborn lamb, he couldn't be further from the truth.'

Matthew went on in the same vein for several more minutes. Ashley gave Victoria her bottle and listened patiently, knowing he would run out of steam sooner or later. His final remark consisted of a somewhat far-fetched correlation between Wayne's dyed hair and his lack of morals.

Said Ashley pacifically, 'I told him I'd call the police——'

'Police? It's nothing to do with the police!' And Matthew was off again.

Ashley put all the authority she could into her voice. 'Grandad, listen to me! It's all very well to talk this way, but Wayne McEvoy is a ruthless and unscrupulous man who's got people like Willie Budgeon on his payroll. I for one do not want to run afoul of Willie. He gives me the creeps.'

'Another bully,' Matthew grumbled.

'Except that Willie, unlike Wayne, isn't afraid to take on someone his own size.'

Matthew glared at her. 'Are you trying to tell me we should sell, Ashley?'

'No. But——'

'Good. For a minute you had me worried. Tell you what we'll do. I'll rig up an alarm system between the garage and the house. And we'll give Tommy some extra hours, so that he's around any time we're open.' A satisfied grin spread over Matthew's face. 'We'll show Wayne McEvoy he can't push us around.'

Ashley gave a sigh of defeat. This whole thing was obviously a huge adventure for Matthew. And, who knows, maybe he was right. Maybe she was being paranoid; motherhood did have a tendency to make one feel excruciatingly vulnerable. So she raised no more objections, and kept out of Matthew's way the morning he installed an ingenious and complicated system of push-buttons and buzzers, worthy of the C.I.A. Her restraint gave out that evening, however, when she discovered Matthew cleaning and polishing his shotgun.

'You're not Wyatt Earp!' she exclaimed. 'And this is Lower Hampton, not the Wild West. Grandad, really . . .'

'I noticed it needed dusting, Ashley,' Matthew said ingenuously. 'Figured I might as well clean it while I had it down from the rack.'

'Just as long as it goes back on the rack—and stays there,' she said grimly. 'I——'

The telephone rang. Ashley picked it up and said crisply, 'Hello.' No one answered. Instead she heard breathing, soft and sibilant, infinitely menacing. Then the connection was cut. Slowly she put down the receiver.

'Who was it?' demanded her grandfather.

'I guess it was a wrong number,' she said uncertainly. She did not believe her own words; but neither did she want to believe in the threat implicit in that waiting silence.

The phone rang twice more that evening. Matthew was in the basement the second time, so Ashley took the call, saying, 'Hello,' with assumed calm. The same breathing pulsed along the line. A man's voice began talking, so quietly and insinuatingly that it took several seconds for his meaning to register. Ashley slammed down the receiver and stood shaking, sickened, and feeling dirty all over.

When the third call came Matthew was stacking up the wood stove for the night and Ashley was rinsing out their tea-cups. 'I'll get it,' she said hurriedly, knowing that, absurdly, she wanted to protect her grandfather from the ugliness of an anonymous caller. When she picked up the receiver, she could not have prevented the animosity in her tone. 'Hello.'

A pause. 'Ashley? Did I get you out of bed?'

Her pent-up breath shuddered in her throat. 'Michael . . . No. No, we're still up.'

'Are you all right?'

'Yes.' Her mind went blank.

'When are you coming to see me?'

'I haven't been invited,' she replied automatically. *What do I do now? Ask how Mary is? Or the detective business?*

'Tomorrow evening?'

'I—I don't know.' *Pull yourself together, Ashley.*

'Do you want to come and see me?' he demanded.

'I don't know that, either.' It was the absolute truth.

From his stance by the woodbox, Matthew was signalling to her. Into the mouthpiece she said, 'Excuse me a minute, Michael . . . What is it, Grandad?'

'You're not to stay home on account of this foolishness with Wayne,' Matthew whispered histrionically. 'I'll cover the home front, don't you worry.'

Eyeing the shotgun, she said wryly, 'That's what I'm afraid of. I don't think I want to go, anyway.'

'Course you do!' Matthew strode across the room, shedding wood chips from his sweater as he went, and grabbed the receiver. 'Michael. Don't pay any attention to her.' He added with low cunning, 'She seems to think I can't handle Victoria now that the child's teething. Women are the greatest worriers in the world, aren't they? Think no kid'll survive without them——'

Her cheeks pink, Ashley said loudly, 'If you're quite finished, Grandad, I might like to continue my conversation.'

In no hurry, Matthew said into the mouthpiece, 'Tomorrow evening, eh? No problem. And drop in yourself, won't you? Always glad to see you. Now, here's Ashley.'

'Thank you, Grandad,' she said, her voice dripping with sarcasm. 'Hello again, Michael. How kind of the two of you to arrange my life for me.'

'Only one evening, Ashley. Come before dark, so I

can show you around the place, then we'll have dinner. See you tomorrow.' And he was gone.

Said Matthew after one look at her face, 'Guess I'd better bring up some more wood from the basement.'

'I think that would be a very wise move.' She watched him scuttle down the stairs, and had to choke back laughter. She was supposed to be angry with him. After all, because of his interference, she was committed to spending an evening with Michael. That should be enough to make her angry ... shouldn't it?

CHAPTER FIVE

THE telephone rang six times in the garage the next morning. Three of the calls were legitimate business calls. Three of them were not. Ashley banged the phone down the first time before the breathing could turn into a voice mouthing obscenities. The second and third time she was not so lucky, for the voice started the moment she'd finished saying, 'MacCulloch's Garage.'

As she went back to replacing a headlight in a Ford Escort, she recognised how horribly vulnerable she was to this tactic of Wayne's; for she had no doubt that he was behind it. She needed the telephone because of her job. She certainly couldn't have an unlisted number. So she was therefore exposed to a kind of harassment that already, in less than twenty-four hours, had her nerves on edge.

Worse was to come. After lunch she had to locate the source of an oil-leak in a half-ton truck that belonged to a crony of Matthew's. She drove the truck into the rear of the garage, and then climbed down the stairs into the narrow, cement-lined pit which was sunk several feet below floor level. Spraying with a solvent under pressure cleaned away the accumulated oil sufficiently that she could start looking for the leak. Turning off the nozzle on the side wall that controlled the air pressure, she reached behind her for the drop light, her ears still ringing with the noise from the jet of air.

The light wasn't on the hook. Frowning, she turned around, and gave an involuntary shriek of alarm. Willie Budgeon was standing behind her in the pit. He had the light in his hand. 'This what you're looking for?' he said softly.

Because of the hiss of air, Ashley hadn't heard his

approach. Her heart hammering away under her overalls, she said composedly, 'Yes, it is,' and reached out her hand to take it.

'You're a cool customer, Ashley MacCulloch. But I reckon I can change that.' He took a step closer.

'What do you want, Willie?' she said boldly. 'Wayne sent you, didn't he? How much is he paying you? Not enough, I bet. You don't build houses like Wayne's by paying your employees a whole lot of money.'

'Yeah, he sent me. Wants me to persuade you to sell the garage. I figured I might enjoy doing that, Ashley.'

He was crowding her into the corner; there was nowhere else to go. 'I don't own the garage—Matthew does.'

'If you get roughed up a bit, Matthew might reconsider.'

She could scream. But the big doors were shut and the odds of Tommy hearing her were slim. Nor had Matthew's alarm system included a buzzer in the pit. Yet if Willie touched her, she knew she would start to scream anyway, regardless of whether anyone would hear her.

He was close enough now that she could see the broken line of a blood vessel in his cheek and a narrow white scar on his lip, as if someone had slashed him with a knife. *Knife ... weapon ...* there must be something she could use as a weapon. Ducking, she grabbed for the nozzle to turn on the air hose. But she was not quick enough. Willie flung her against the wall, knocking the breath from her body. His hand caught her across the cheekbone. Then he was gripping her arms, his fingernails like claws digging through her sweater as his mouth ground against hers.

She kicked out viciously with her steel-toed boot. Willie grunted with pain, loosening his hold. Above them a man's voice called plaintively, 'Is anyone around?'

Ashley twisted her head free, filling her lungs with air. 'I'll be right there!' she yelped.

Willie looked as if he would like to strangle her on the spot. She pushed herself away from the wall, feeling her knees tremble under her, and began to edge past him. He seized her wrist in one hand and twisted it cruelly, watching her flinch with pain. 'Next time I'll make sure nobody comes,' he grated, and dropped her wrist.

Climbing the seven stairs to the ground level was like climbing a mountain. Wondering if she was going to faint, Ashley walked round the corner and came face to face with Mr Darby, husband of the redoubtable Emma. Not for anything did she want Emma Darby to know what had just happened, because it would only confirm Emma's prejudices about girls who worked in garages. She took a deep breath. 'Sorry I kept you waiting, Mr Darby, I didn't hear you,' she said with perfect truth.

'Hope you didn't mind me walking in—the young fellow said it would be all right.'

She gave him a dazzling smile. 'Not at all, believe me. Can I help you?'

'Little problem with the signal light. Could it be a fuse?' He blinked at her anxiously. 'I hate to bother you.'

Poor Mr Darby, he was always apologising for something. 'It won't take a minute to check. I'll open the door for you, and you can drive the car inside.' As she did so, Willie brushed past her, not looking at her or saying a word; he got into his truck which he had parked on the far side of the garage out of sight of the house, and drove off. Ashley's body sagged against the door frame. He had gone ... but he would be back. They both knew that.

She replaced the fuse for Mr Darby, then went back into the pit to work on the truck, conquering the cowardly impulse to keep looking back over her shoulder every two or three minutes. At three-thirty when she had finished she walked over to the house, leaving Tommy in charge. Her grandfather and Victoria

were out in the garden, Victoria seated in her pram
supervising Matthew as he raked leaves, a role that
appeared to suit them both. Ashley played with her
daughter for a few minutes, hoping it would ease some
of her inner tension. But it achieved the reverse,
accentuating her unspoken terror that somehow Wayne
or Willie would harm the baby.

Maybe a hot shower would help, she thought
miserably, replacing Victoria in the carriage with a kiss
on her downy-soft cheek. But although she consciously
attempted to relax as she showered and dressed, she
could feel the tension still singing along her nerves when
she finally went downstairs. In the kitchen, where he
was washing his hands, Matthew gave an appreciative
whistle. 'Very nice,' he said. 'Very nice indeed.'

She was wearing a flared plaid skirt in shades of
forest green with a cream long-sleeved blouse and a
knitted vest of mohair, her hair in a single thick plait
tied with dark green ribbon. Her make-up was more
heavily applied than usual in an effort to hide the blue
shadows under her eyes and the reddened skin over her
cheekbone; Matthew noticed nothing amiss, so she
must have been successful. Pulling on dark brown knee-
high boots and a raincoat, she said, 'Your friends are
arriving any minute, aren't they, Grandad?'

'That's right. I must get the card table out.' These
weekly evening card games, which rotated from house
to house, were ostensibly for whist or auction forty-
fives; Ashley harboured the unworthy suspicion that as
soon as the various womenfolk were out of the way a
particularly virulent form of poker was substituted. As
long as Matthew had company this evening, they could
play strip poker for all she cared.

'I won't be late,' she said. 'Nobody leaves before
midnight, do they?'

'Only at Bessie Somers'.'

Bessie was a friend of Emma Darby's. Ashley gave a
reluctant grin. 'Take care, Grandad. 'Bye, Victoria.'

Her grandfather's car was a secondhand Honda

which he had shamefully neglected, but which Ashley had brought to a state of purring docility. She drove the forty-odd miles to Michael's farm in a state of suspended animation, absently admiring the tree-clad hills, the shadowed valleys where streams meandered to the distant sea, and the golden splendour of the sinking sun. None of it really touched her. Nothing had, since Willie's brutal assault. He had touched her, she thought grimly. In a very literal way. How was she to defend herself and her family from him?

She was so absorbed in her thoughts that she almost missed the turn-off, marked by a simple white sign that said *Valleyview Farm*. The driveway, unpaved, wound alongside a rock-strewn brook, the road in no more hurry to reach its destination than was the brook. Trying to pull herself together, Ashley began paying more attention to her surroundings. She rolled down the window, hearing the water chuckle between the moss-covered boulders and the clear sharp whistle of a bird hidden deep in the undergrowth. It was very peaceful, very beautiful; the garage seemed a long way away.

The road began to climb. When she emerged from the woods into a clearing she saw the house immediately. It was built on the slope of the hill in the midst of a grove of maple and elm trees, smoke rising lazily from its chimneys, the yellow glow of lighted windows offering a welcome to the traveller. It was an old-fashioned saltbox house, grey-painted with white trim, enlarged by a wing to the south and an attached garage; its proportions had the grace and dignity of a more prosperous and leisurely era. It was much more substantial than Ashley had subconsciously expected, presenting a whole new aspect to the Michael she knew with his ancient jeep and his lumberman's jacket.

The driveway curved to the left to a parking area under the trees. From the corner of her eye she saw Michael come out of a side door and run down the steps, and knew he must have been watching for her arrival. She felt a moment of wild and unreasoning happiness, as pure a gold as the westering sky. Parking the car beside his battered jeep, she climbed out, closing the door. To her right a sparrow gave its piercing four-note whistle. Casually she glanced that way and her heart stopped. Parked on the far side of the jeep was a shiny black Mercedes. Mary Gibson's car; Ashley would have recognised it anywhere.

Something in her snapped. She whirled. Michael was hurrying across the gravel towards her. He was smiling ... *smiling*. How dared he! She grabbed for the handle and swung the door of the Honda open again, throwing her handbag on the passenger seat and fumbling in the pocket of her raincoat for her keys.

'Ashley! How good to see you.' His voice changed. 'What's wrong?'

She was shaking all over, consumed by rage. 'I'm going home,' she announced, her eyes glittering.

'What the hell——' He grabbed her arm.

She shook herself free. 'Let *go* of me!'

'What the devil are you playing at?'

'What were you planning to do?' she hissed. 'Hide her upstairs and keep me downstairs? Or were we going to have a delightful evening *à trois*! Michael and his harem ... Well, you can damn well count me out!'

'Shut *up*!'

There was so much violence in the two little words that momentarily Ashley was shocked into obeying him. He said between gritted teeth, 'Now will you please explain to me what the hell you're ranting on about?'

'Oh, I'll explain all right.' Her voice broke. 'Although I wish you'd give up this—this farcical pretence that everything is as it should be. If you want to go out with Mary Gibson, Michael, you go right ahead—but leave me out of it. I'm not into sharing. Mary one night, me the next. . . . How do you think I feel when I come here to see you and find that blasted Mercedes parked next to your jeep?'

He followed the direction of her gaze, saw the
Mercedes and said with an air of faint surprise that
infuriated Ashley still further, 'Oh, Mary's here, is she?
I didn't realise she was coming today.'

'Perhaps you should get a social secretary to keep
your dates straight,' Ashley said viciously. 'Goodbye,
Michael.'

'I do believe you're jealous.'

Halfway into the Honda, she threw him a scathing
glance. 'Jealous? Don't flatter yourself!'

'Mary is not and never has been my—er—girl-friend.'

She straightened, her green skirt swirling around her
legs. 'Oh, sure—that's not what you told me earlier.'

'I never at any time told you I was involved in a
romantic liaison with Mary.'

'You certainly implied that you were, that first
evening we met.'

'You made certain assumptions which I didn't deny.
If we're going to have a fight, let's at least be accurate,
Ashley.'

'Why didn't you deny them?' she lashed back. 'And
why is she here this evening?'

Piercingly sweet, the sparrow called again. 'Let's just
say that I was in a state of shock that first evening,'
Michael answered slowly. 'I'd met this skinny, bad-
tempered kid who looked like a boy, and who then
proceeded to offer me the hospitality of her home and
to bewitch me with her hair like silk and her eyes like
clouds in an autumn sky . . . when she held her child at
her breast, her love shone like a ray of sunlight through
the clouds.'

Physically he was not touching her. Yet his words
awoke a wild, sweet longing within her, a hunger for
more. She said wonderingly, 'You mean—me?'

'Yes, I mean you.' Abruptly descending to more
mundane matters, Michael added, 'Mary works for me
part-time. She's a social worker based in Halifax and
comes here two or three times a week to see two of the
boys who are from the Halifax area. As far as I know,

she's in love with a young doctor who's going into psychiatry—which will be a most suitable match.'

Ashley's jaw dropped. 'Oh,' she said inadequately. 'Really?'

'Really.' His smile was wider. 'So now do I get a kiss?'

She looked up at him, her eyes a confusion of different emotions, her lips a soft, vulnerable curve. 'I guess so.'

He took her in his arms with a deliberation that made her tremble, and bent his head to hers. Still under the spell of his words, she responded with a touching trust, sliding her arms around his neck and offering him her lips. His kiss deepened, demanding more, and she gave with a generosity that inflamed him. As she felt the first dizzying touch of his tongue, she buried her fingers in his thick, springing hair, and gave herself up to the sweetness of an exploration that made her shiver with pleasure. Then his hand slid to the softness of her breast and her entrancement was shattered. Just so had David touched her many months ago, and what had followed had brought her pain and the ache of unfulfilment ... she pulled away, her body tense, the wonder fading from her face. 'No, Michael——'

'I'm sorry—am I going too fast for you? You must know I want you.'

She stepped back, shoving her hands in her pockets, and gratefully seized upon the excuse he had given her. 'Yes, you're going too fast.'

He seemed to accept her words at face value. Kissing her cheek, he said, 'Why don't you get your handbag out of the car and I'll take you on the grand tour before it gets too dark to see anything?'

Ashley flushed, remembering why her purse had ended up where it was. 'I'm sorry I lost my temper.'

'No problem,' he responded with undeniable smugness.

'I wasn't jealous,' she said defensively.

'Of course you weren't.' He took her hand. 'Come along.'

His fingers, curling around hers, were warm and strong. She said with a pertness that sounded almost convincing, 'Where do we start? I want to see the famous Cheviot-Corriedales or whatever they are.'

'Plain Cheviots. I'm thinking of getting some crossbreeds next year.'

They walked past the front of the house and down a tree-shaded lane to a collection of sheds and barns. Grassy meadows dotted with grazing sheep spread down the hillside to the wooded valley, and then up the far slope again. 'The sheep are kept outside a good part of the year,' Michael remarked. 'In winter they shelter in the sheds and we put up snow fencing for added protection. Part of the programme with the boys who live here is that they do some of the farm work. We built that far shed, the new one, see? And the boys help bring in the winter supply of wood and look after the garden. In the summer I organise backpacking trips which include survival in the woods, basic map-reading and compass orientation. It all seems to help.'

It was Ashley's first opportunity to learn more about an aspect of Michael's life that intrigued her. 'How many boys are here?' she asked.

'Eleven at the moment. They come and go, although I try to keep each boy at least twelve months. They range in age from ten to seventeen.'

'Why are they here?'

'Trouble with the law, generally. Quite a few are on probation, although occasionally we're sent a kid who can't settle in a foster-home anywhere. I don't want you to think we work any miracles, Ashley. The failure rate is about equal to the success rate. But for some boys this place works, and you see a young fellow who was headed for a sure prison sentence starting again on a new track—and that makes up for all the failures. I don't do it by myself, by the way. There's a full-time teacher and two part-time social workers, one of whom is Mary, as well as a housekeeper, Beth Collins. I look after most of the outdoors stuff.'

The sky had darkened to a lurid display of orange and purple, the kind of sky that if painted would look indescribably vulgar. Ashley said slowly, 'It's all much more impressive than I expected. You must be rich, Michael.'

'I inherited money from my father,' he said briefly. 'Seen enough?'

Forbidden ground obviously, she thought as they started back towards the house.

A light was shining from a small aluminium-covered shed on their right. Michael said uncertainly, 'Hold it a minute—looks as though someone left the light on.' She trailed after him, and as he opened the door heard him say, 'Hello, Tim—what are you up to?' He stepped inside.

Curious, Ashley followed him, standing in the doorway. A small boy with flaming red hair and truculent grey eyes was crouched on the floor amid a litter of engine parts.

'Trying to fix it,' the boy said to Michael, his tone bordering on insolence.

He had taken apart the motor of a garden tiller. Taken it apart with great thoroughness, Ashley noticed. 'What was the trouble?' she asked.

The boy looked at her as if he would have expected such a question from a woman. 'It won't go.'

The floor of the shed was cement, and relatively clean. She knelt down, picking up the spark plug. 'That could do with cleaning, but it's in relatively good shape,' she said reflectively. 'The air cleaner's dirty, although that probably wouldn't affect the starting. Do you know how to clean it?'

'No—do you?' the boy asked rudely.

He plainly expected her to say no. She said calmly, 'My name is Ashley. What's yours?'

'Tim.'

'Well, I do know how, actually, Tim. You have to wash this sponge in liquid detergent and water, squeeze it as dry as you can, and then saturate it in oil. If you run the machine with the sponge as filthy as this, you'll get dirt abrading the engine.'

'How do you know all that?' demanded Tim suspiciously.

Very conscious of Michael standing to one side listening to every word and somehow knowing he was pleased with the interchange, she said, peering at a connection stud, 'I'm a licensed mechanic. I work in a garage. There's your problem.'

'Yeah?'

A young man of few words, was Tim. 'The contact area is corroded. Have you got a bit of sandpaper?' He fished in the toolbox that was beside him and produced a small square. 'If you scrape the rust off these brackets, then you'll have a good connection.'

Tim scraped away industriously for a minute or two. Finally he held the terminal up for inspection. 'Would that be all right?'

He was asking her opinion; from the few brief minutes Ashley had spent in Tim's company she sensed this might be a major breakthrough. 'That should do it. You know, by the look of this machine, it hasn't been getting regular maintenance. Maybe tomorrow if you had time you could get it started and let it run for at least three-quarters of an hour. That would re-charge the battery.'

Tim looked warily at Michael, who said, 'As long as it's after classes, Tim.'

Looking at the strewn nuts and bolts, Ashley said noncommittally, 'You'll remember how to put it together again, Tim?'

'Course I will.' Tim looked at her through lashes that were as thick as a girl's. 'Are you really a mechanic? That's a man's job.'

'But there's no reason a woman can't do it. You see, I grew up with four brothers, Tim, who were always pulling motors apart. They had an old sports car that they kept in the garage ... by the time I was twelve I knew all there was to know about the engine of that car.' She smiled reminiscently. 'Because my hands are small, I used to be better at some things than my brothers—they didn't like that!'

'Nobody's ever showed me,' said Tim.

He wouldn't ask, she knew. She said carefully, 'If it's all right with Mr Gault, maybe he could bring you to my garage some Saturday and you can work along with me.'

She might have imagined the flare of interest in the grey eyes, so quickly was it masked. 'Maybe,' Tim said stonily.

Ashley got to her feet. Michael said, 'I'll lock the shed now, Tim, it's time for supper. You can get the key from me tomorrow afternoon.'

Head downbent, Tim preceded them outdoors, then dashed off towards the house like a rock from a catapult. No thanks, no goodbyes, Ashley noticed. She turned to Michael. 'I hope you didn't mind me inviting him to the garage.'

'It might be a good thing—get his interest. It's the first indication I've had of something he likes. Tim's only been here three months, Ashley, and he's already run away twice. He hasn't yet learned that there's nowhere for him to run.'

She remembered the closed-in little face and the belligerent eyes. 'Why is he here?' she asked.

'He's illegitimate. It's doubtful if his mother ever knew who his father was. She kept Tim for two and a half years, but then he had to be taken from her—because of neglect.'

'Neglect?' Ashley said doubtfully. 'But wouldn't he have been better off with his mother?'

'Not in this case. He was half-starved, Ashley. Suffering from severe malnutrition is what the report said. After he was taken from his mother, he unfortunately went from foster-home to foster-home, and started running away on a regular basis about four years ago. He's ten now. He's never known anything permanent, so he's afraid to trust in anyone or anything. Certainly he's afraid to love anyone.'

'Oh, Michael...' She thought of Victoria, also illegitimate, but protected and loved from the moment of her birth. 'I can't understand how a mother could mistreat her child.'

'Perhaps because she was mistreated herself, Ashley. It's one of those clouded areas where it's all too easy to be judgemental and all too hard to understand. But try and see it from her point of view. She was very young and dirt-poor. No regular job, and no training whatsoever for being a mother... All we can hope is that Tim will settle down here and some of the damage can be undone.'

The sun had set and the light was fading fast. As they started back to the house Michael added matter-of-factly, 'The boys will be eating now, you can meet them another time. I have a wing of the house for myself, so we'll go there.'

But as they passed the big front door with its fan light and brass lantern, the door opened and a woman hurried out. 'Michael!' she called. 'I'm glad I caught you.' She ran lightly down the steps, her russet hair swinging around her ears.

Deliberately Michael put his arm around Ashley. 'Mary, I'd like you to meet Ashley MacCulloch,' he said easily. 'Ashley, Mary Gibson.'

As the two women smiled and shook hands, it was obvious to Ashley that Mary did not recognise her. They exchanged a few commonplaces, then Mary said, 'I'll be away for three days next week, Michael. If you should need anyone, Peter Trenholm is on call.'

'Taking off with the doctor?' Michael teased.

'No such luck! No, my sister's getting married in Ontario.' She glanced at her watch. 'But I am meeting Roger on his break tonight, so I'd better go. Nice to have met you, Ashley. 'Bye, Michael.' She hurried across the gravel to the Mercedes.

There had been nothing remotely lover-like in the exchange between Michael and Mary. Ashley felt her heart lighten and said generously, 'She's very beautiful.'

'I suppose she is.' His arm tightened and he leered at her. 'I prefer blondes myself.'

'At any moment you're going to suggest I should see your etchings!'

'That's passé, Ashley. I shall simply ply you with strong drink.'

'And a meal?' she said hopefully.

'So it's my cooking you're after, not my body.'

She lowered her eyes, the joke no longer a joke. 'Michael——'

'Come along. Oysters Rockefeller, beef Stroganoff, and chocolate mousse—will that do?'

'It sounds wonderful,' she said helplessly, allowing herself to be ushered in the side door.

Michael's wing of the house was more spacious than her grandfather's whole house. A curved staircase swept up from the foyer, whose polished oak floor was partly covered by an exquisite, richly-toned Persian carpet. The sunken living-room had a massive stone fireplace and what must be a glorious view of the surrounding hills, while the kitchen, complete with a south-facing solarium, combined a highly efficient layout and the most expensive of appliances with the charm of pine cupboards and stained glass windows. The Stroganoff smelled delicious.

Michael turned on a fluorescent light over the sink. 'Do you want to get a couple of glasses out of the cupboard while I put on the rice?'

Ashley reached up into the cupboard. The glasses were lead crystal and exquisitely carved; she held one up to the light, admiring the ever-changing rainbow of colours in the depths of the crystal. Michael said sharply, 'You've bruised your cheek.'

She almost dropped the glass. Looking the picture of guilt, she stammered, 'Oh—oh, yes.'

'How did that happen?'

Willie took a crack at me . . . But she couldn't say that. Although in this beautiful house set in the forest-clad hills Wayne McEvoy might seem a very long way away, because of Victoria and Matthew she could not afford to take any risks. She said, still staring at the glass, 'Victoria was waving one of her toys in the air and caught me on the cheek. It was my own fault.'

'You're lying, Ashley.'

Her eyes snapped up. She said with just the right touch of irritation, 'Don't be silly—why should I lie? Where do you keep all this strong drink you were talking about?'

His gaze was disconcertingly level, and she knew he still disbelieved her. But all he said was, 'The right-hand cupboard under the counter,' and she let out her breath in a tiny sigh of relief. Wanting to distract him, she added, 'You know, you've never told me what you used to do before you bought this place?'

She had succeeded in her aim. His face tightened. 'I'll have a Scotch and soda,' he said. 'Help yourself to whatever you want, there's mix in the refrigerator.' His back was towards her as he measured rice into a bowl. 'I was a policeman.'

'Oh? Whereabouts?'

'Toronto. Montreal. Vancouver.'

She had to ask it. 'What made you leave?'

'The knee injury. Oh, they gave me a nice safe desk job in Regina, but it was driving me crazy. So I got out.'

Measuring the whisky, she said provocatively, 'You mean you used to direct traffic? And give people speeding tickets?'

'Not quite,' he said drily, taking a metal tray of oysters out of the refrigerator. 'For most of the time I was an undercover agent in the narcotics division.'

Ashley gave up any pretence of preparing their drinks. 'So that's what you meant when you said you'd seen so much of human greed and cruelty.'

'It's a dirty business, drug-dealing. There are no heroes. Least of all, me.'

She winced at the bitterness in his voice. 'Why do you say that?'

'I don't want you getting an image of me as the good guy on the side of the law, always doing right. Fighting fearlessly against the forces of evil. It was never that simple.' He seemed to have forgotten her presence, his hands gripping the edge of the counter. 'Is it right to arrest a kid who's screaming for his fix, knowing the hell he'll suffer in withdrawal symptoms? And what about the small-time dealer, the guy on the street corner who's never known anything but grinding poverty, and who sees this as a way to get a bit of money? Money he feels entitled to. Money that middle class citizens take for granted, as their right . . . It's the big men you want to get, the men who run the show. And that's just about impossible.'

'You tried,' she said passionately, 'which is more than most of us do. And you cared about those others, didn't you? The kids on heroin, the junkies . . .'

'I suppose I did.'

'I know you did.' She knew something else: that Wayne had lied to her when he had said Michael had been dishonourably discharged. She had suspected as much, but now she was sure. 'How did you get your knee hurt?'

'You don't want to know about that, Ashley.' He shifted restlessly. 'I hardly ever talk about those days any more. If I am to you now, it's because you're becoming very important to me, so I want you to know the truth.'

His words both frightened and exhilarated her. 'Then tell me about your knee,' she said evenly.

To her surprise he obeyed her. 'I blew my cover, so I got caught. They tied me up and shot me in the kneecap.' He grimaced. 'I was lucky they didn't blow my head off. Lucky, too, that they went away and left me to bleed to death and that my cohort tracked me down before I did.'

Ashley's imagination, often too vivid for her own good, could supply all the ugly details he had omitted. She crossed the room and put her arms around him, holding him as tightly as she could, her face buried in his shirtfront. 'I'm so glad you were found,' she whispered shakily. 'What a horrible way it would have been to die . . . all alone like that!'

Michael raised her face in his hands, his expression both quizzical and tender. 'You're crying.'

She wiped at her eyes, smudging her carefully applied mascara. 'No, I'm not,' she gulped.

He kissed the tiny droplet trickling down her cheek, then his lips moved to her mouth. For Ashley there was no holding back this time, no hesitation. Fiercely she kissed him back, exulting in the hard strength of his body, as all the generosity and passion of which she was capable was tapped for the first time in her life.

When they eventually separated, she could hear the harsh rhythm of his breathing; it echoed her own. Everything was the same: the pleasant kitchen, the food on the counter, the two occupants. Yet nothing was the same. Hands on his chest, she suddenly pushed herself away from him. 'I—I don't understand,' she said raggedly. 'I'm not like——' She could not finish the sentence.

'I don't think you know what you're like. At least as far as sex is concerned.' As she flushed like a young girl, his face gentled. 'The man who's Victoria's father—was he good to you?'

The flush deepened to two hectic patches of colour. She knew what he meant. *Did you enjoy sex with David?* That was what he meant. But how could she admit to the truth? That her awkwardness, inexperience and pain had ruined what is surely supposed to be a glorious and earth-shattering encounter?

Michael was still watching her. She sought for something to say. 'Of course he was good to me. He loved me, didn't he?'

'I would doubt it. As do you, Ashley.' As if he had got the answer he wanted, he said, 'Now, are you going to pour me that drink?'

'You're an exasperating man!' she exclaimed, recklessly sloshing rum into her glass. She could have added other adjectives. Like disturbing, attractive and intense . . . frighteningly intense. They would all suit him. But these she kept to herself, just as she was keeping to herself a number of questions about David. Had he been good to her? Or had he been a hurried and crude lover, so selfish that her pleasure—or lack of it—had not interested him? They were unanswerable questions, for she had no basis for comparison, and her own self-confidence had sustained such a blow that she was incapable of objectivity.

Michael had begun a witty discourse on the origins of Scotch whisky, and soon she was laughing with him, thoroughly enjoying herself, the shadows banished. They ate in the dining room, where the cathedral ceiling was pierced by skylights and the floor covered by lushly soft wool carpeting. After the meal Michael lit a fire in the stone fireplace in the living-room and they drank coffee and liqueurs and listened to Sibelius. They were seated side by side on a deep, soft chesterfield covered in a dark polished cotton; Ashley had wondered if she might have to fight Michael off, but he scrupulously kept a couple of feet between them, making no move to touch her. Contrarily she found herself piqued that this should be so.

When he got up to get more coffee, she followed him into the kitchen. 'We seem to have made an awful mess,' she commented, looking around at the dirty plates and cutlery and the scraps of leftover food. 'Why don't I help you clean up?'

'No need, Ashley, I've got a dishwasher.'

'It still has to be loaded.' Somehow she did not want to return to the comfort of the chesterfield in front of the flickering fire, and the slow, sensual music. 'It won't take long.' She rolled up her sleeves and rinsed off a dinner plate, and for a few minutes they worked in a companionable silence. Then Michael moved over to the sink to clean out a saucepan, passing her an empty dish as he did so. She took it, about to say, 'You have such beautiful china,' when he circled her wrist with his hand and said grimly, 'Victoria didn't do that.'

There were two abrasions on her skin and a reddened area where Willie had twisted her arm. She said tightly, 'Michael, I do wish you'd mind your own business.'

'You are my business.'

With exaggerated care she placed the Royal Doulton vegetable dish on the counter. 'Just what do you mean by that?'

He hesitated, his fingers still clasping her wrist. 'I'm not sure I can—or want to—explain right now,' he said finally. 'I do know that I like you, Ashley——'

'What about Becky-Cynthia?' she interrupted, hoping to distract him. 'You don't like her.'

He smiled suddenly, and to her annoyance her heart did a flip-flop in her breast. 'I'm seeing less and less of her, it seems.'

'She's still very much around—so don't count on it.'

'Oh, she adds a little spice to life.'

'Let's finish cleaning up. I've got to go home.'

'I hadn't finished what I was saying.'

'I don't think I want to hear it.'

'Too bad,' he said, not sounding as if he liked her at all, Ashley noticed. 'I want to keep on seeing you. I might even be falling in love with you.' She drew back, paling visibly. 'I certainly desire you,' he finished. 'That's not telling you anything you don't already know.'

She tugged her wrist free. 'I don't want to hear any more!'

'Why not?' he demanded, his eyes an angry blue. 'What are you scared of, Ashley?'

'You don't want me,' she cried incoherently. 'How could you? I'm not a virgin—I have a child, an illegitimate child. I'm used goods, Michael. Why would you want me?'

'There are ways and ways of being used—believe me, I've seen them all. When are you going to let up on yourself? Forgive yourself for one mistake?'

'My parents disowned me for that mistake! I disgraced them—they said so.'

'Do you agree with them?' he rapped.

Her anger evaporated. '*I* don't know.'

'Let me tell you how I see it, Ashley MacCulloch. Do you know what I think would have been a disgrace?' Wordlessly she shook her head. 'If you'd allowed them to talk you into an abortion when you didn't want one. Or if you'd given up the baby against every instinct in you. But you didn't do either of those things, did you? You were too stubborn and too courageous and too true to yourself. You did what you felt was right—and that's all any of us can do. So for God's sake, stop downgrading yourself.'

She was standing with her mouth open. 'I never thought of it that way before.'

'Then it's time you did.'

'And you're right—I have been going around apologising for myself, haven't I?'

'Sure you have. Telling everyone you're an unmarried mother so they'll be sure to cross the road when they see you coming ... Get this straight, Ashley—when I say I want you, I mean every word of it. You're a beautiful woman, and that's part of the reason. But I also want you because you're the way you are—a fighter. Brave as a lion and pig-headed as a mule.'

She gave him a wondering smile. 'How very unromantic!'

'Oh, I can be romantic.' Michael put down the saucepan and walked up to her. She held her ground. He untied the velvet ribbon that bound her hair and unwound it from its braid, spreading it in a pale cloud around her shoulders and bringing two shining strands forward to cover her breasts. She quivered as his hands brushed the softness of her flesh. He said huskily, 'One day I'll do that to you when you're naked. Then I'll caress your breasts with my hands tangled in your hair and you'll bend to my touch as the ripe grain bends to the wind.'

She said very quietly, 'And you wouldn't mind that you were not the first?'

'No. Because I'd make you mine in a way he never did. And I would give you such pleasure that you would hear your own voice crying out with joy.'

She seemed to shrink in his arms. 'But it's not like that for me,' she whispered, staring at his shirt.

'You mean with David it wasn't like that?'

'No. I hated it!' she burst out. 'It hurt and—and I didn't feel any different. I think maybe I'm frigid. Isn't that what they call women like me?' She risked an upward glance at him through her lashes. If she had expected to see disappointment or dismay, or even withdrawal, she was disappointed. Instead Michael looked as if he was holding on to his temper with considerable difficulty. Ashley tried to pull away, saying pathetically, 'Are you angry with me?'

'I'd like to beat your David to a pulp.'

'He's not my David,' was the only reply she could think of.

'Thank God for that! Ashley, if that's the way he left you feeling, then he was an insensitive, selfish clod. How he ever had the nerve to tell you he loved you, I'll never know. Because loving is giving—that's basic. It doesn't sound as if he gave you very much.'

'He gave me a child.'

'But none of the passion and splendour that can go into creating a child.'

'No . . . none of that.'

'It would be different with me, Ashley. Because to give you pleasure would make me deeply happy.'

She stood very still, her head whirling. Could it be true? It was David himself who had used that horrible word frigid to her. Had he been right? Or had it been that his lovemaking had indeed been hurried and rough and totally insensitive to her needs—something she, in her inexperience, had not understood. She said uncertainly, 'I have to think about all this. Maybe you're right . . .'

Wisely Michael let his hands drop to his sides. 'Back to the dishpan?' he said lightly.

'I guess so.' She was very silent as they finished cleaning up the kitchen and quite unaware that Michael was watching her. When the last saucepan had been put away, she said, 'I think I'd better go, Michael. Grandad will wait up for me, so I don't want to be too late.'

'All right. May I come and see you in a couple of days? Say Saturday evening?'

'Yes,' she said simply. 'I'd like that.'

'Good. I'll get your coat.'

He walked her out to the car. It was dark under the trees, the nip of frost in the air. Opening her door, Michael looked down on the pale oval of her face. 'Will you do me a favour, Ashley?'

It never occurred to her to refuse. 'Of course.'

'I'd like you to do something for me. I'd like you to kiss me goodnight as if you were in love with me. Don't think of David or Victoria or your parents. Only of me—the man you love and would like to give pleasure to.'

She gazed at him in silence. His eyes were shadowed pits, his expression inscrutable, and for a moment all the old fears came back. She didn't love him. She dared not love him, for she had loved David and look what had happened ... although David, she realised painfully, had never treated her with as much care and integrity as Michael had. Slowly she slid her arms around Michael's neck, closed her eyes, and allowed herself to imagine that she was in love with him.

Standing on tiptoes, she brushed her lips down his cheek to his mouth, running her fingers through his hair and caressing the nape of his neck. Very delicately she traced the line of his mouth with her tongue, then took his lower lip in her teeth, teasing it gently. Then she slid her tongue between his teeth, moving her mouth slowly and sensuously against his, her one desire to bring him pleasure. Her body, pliant as the long summer grass in the wind, swayed against him. Because her coat was unbuttoned she could feel his tautly muscled chest against the swell of her breasts.

He had been standing almost passively until now. But as though the softness of her flesh had inflamed him, he groaned her name, and then his own tongue touched hers, flooding her whole body with sweetness. His hands slid down her back, drawing her so close to him that she could feel his arousal. Symbol of his need and desire . . . but also of his inevitable demand, his ultimate invasion of her.

The brief, beautiful world of illusion was instantly destroyed. Ashley pulled away, her eyes wide with panic. 'Don't, Michael . . . please, don't!'

For a terrified instant she was sure he was not going to obey her. Then his hands loosened their hold. His voice was blurred with desire. 'Did I hurt you?'

'No—you frightened me.'

'You don't have to be frightened of me, Ashley.'

Her head was a jumble of conflicting thoughts and emotions. The bittersweet ache of longing she had felt when she had kissed him had been almost as powerful as the fear that had conquered it. Once again she had discovered how capable Michael was of tenderness and solicitude . . . but equally she knew him for a tough, virile man who had lived a dangerous life and would know better than most how to take what he wanted. And at the moment what he wanted was herself, she was in no doubt about that.

Hopelessly confused, she mumbled, 'I'd better go. Thank you, Michael, it was a lovely evening.'

He slowly expelled his breath from between his teeth. 'One day you'll stop running,' he said heavily.

She could think of nothing to say. Slipping free of him, she seated herself in the Honda, searching for the ignition key in her pocket.

His, 'Goodnight. I'll see you Saturday,' was spoken in a voice devoid of emotion. As she drove away the single clear thought that surfaced in her brain was that he had forgotten to pursue the subject of her injured wrist; she had not had to mention Willie's name. For that she was grateful. For the rest, she scarcely knew what to think.

CHAPTER SIX

AT eight o'clock the next morning Tommy arrived on the doorstep wearing that look of mingled apprehension and excitement that signifies the bearer of bad news. 'Someone's stolen some gas!' he exclaimed to Ashley. 'They cut through the padlocks.'

Ashley stared at him in consternation. Every evening the motors on the gas pumps were switched off inside the office, and as a further precaution the nozzles were padlocked to the tanks. But if the nozzles were free and the thief had even a small hand pump, he could steal gallons of gasoline direct from the underground storage tanks.

She dragged on her jacket and pushed her feet into her boots, following Tommy across the grass. The padlocks had been cut with a hacksaw, she saw, staring at the now useless bits of metal in total frustration. And she'd be willing to bet that Wayne McEvoy was behind this. He wouldn't have done it himself—not Wayne. But he was the instigator.

When she dipped into the storage tanks, she discovered that the total loss was slightly over two hundred gallons. Not a devastating loss, by any means, but bad enough at today's prices. She did not think that the object of the theft had been to reduce her and her grandfather to instant bankruptcy; rather it had been a way of pointing out their vulnerability to attack. Wayne could act with impunity: that was the message.

She walked back to the house and relayed the information to Matthew. He did not take it quietly; she had not expected that he would. When he had prowled around the kitchen swearing vengeance and railing against Wayne for long enough, she said levelly, 'I'll leave the outside lights on tonight.' Her grandfather had installed two large arc lamps over the gas pumps a couple of years ago.

'Locking the stable door after the horse is gone!' he roared.

'At least the other horses won't get stolen.'

'We're not going to call the police,' Matthew announced belligerently.

'We're playing right into his hands, aren't we?' she said bitterly. 'Grandad, you don't think we should just sell and get out now, before anything worse happens? He holds all the cards, you know.'

'I've got a few tricks up my sleeve yet, Ashley.'

The telephone rang. Matthew grabbed the receiver before Ashley could and after a couple of seconds banged it back on the hook in disgust. 'No one there. That happened a couple of times last night as well.'

She might as well tell him. 'They're waiting for me to pick up the phone,' she said with attempted lightness. 'Obscene phone calls—you've heard of them?'

'You mean . . .? That bastard wouldn't——'

'He would and he has. I didn't tell you because I knew you'd be upset.'

'*Upset?* I'll wring his neck!'

Victoria, who had been watching Matthew's per-ambulations with fascination, banged her rattle on the high chair, crowing her approval.

A reluctant smile pulled at Matthew's mouth. 'Bloodthirsty little wretch,' he grumbled.

'A chip off the old block, Grandad.'

Matthew gave a complacent grin, his temper forgotten, then said briskly, 'Okay. From now on I'll answer the phone around here. I'll give 'em obscenities if that's what they want. We'll leave every outdoor light on that we own. And don't you go hiding things from me, my girl.'

Ashley said with a diplomatic mixture of truth and untruth, 'You know, it occurred to me yesterday that there's no alarm bell in the pit. Would it be very difficult to install one there?'

'Good idea,' Matthew said sagely. 'We must cover all the angles.'

'You're enjoying this, aren't you?' Ashley accused.

'Must admit it adds a little pep to life.'

It was her turn to be direct. 'You keep a close eye on Victoria, Grandad. I'm serious.'

It was no accident that Matthew's eye wandered to the newly polished shotgun on its rack high on the wall. 'Sure will.'

Matthew had read far too many detective stories. Ashley gave a sigh of resignation. 'I'd better go to work,' she said.

Four of the dozen or so phone calls at the garage that day were her anonymous enemy. She could never get the receiver down quite quickly enough, and was always left with the echo of a whispered phrase that filled her with revulsion and helpless rage. But Willie came nowhere near the garage, and the night was uneventful.

However, on Friday Ashley had to run a few errands. She walked to the post office, then made her bank deposits. Coming out of the bank she stood for a moment to one side of the paved walk, dimly aware of the people coming and going and of vehicles drawing into the parking lot. Her brow furrowed, she ran her eyes over the latest statement of credits and debits. There was more money then she had expected in her current account.

A hand took her by the elbow, and startled, she looked up into Willie's pale eyes. She shoved the statement back into its envelope and snapped, 'Let go, Willie! I don't ever want to see you again.'

She might as well have saved her breath. 'Sure, I'll run you home,' he said loudly.

'No, thanks,' she hissed, knowing perfectly well what he was up to. He was going to make a scene in front of half the villagers.

He put his arm around her, and almost lifting her off her feet began steering her towards his new red truck. 'How've you been? We had a good time the other night, didn't we?'

It was his self-assurance that did it, his certainty that she would give in and go with him to avoid embarrassment. She announced loudly enough to be heard across the street, 'I don't want a drive, Willie. Put me down!'

He laughed coarsely, his hand biting into her hip. 'You were willing enough the other night.'

They were only a few feet from the truck. Suddenly terrified that his crude antics were going to succeed, and knowing if she did get in the truck with him they would not be going to the garage, Ashley dug her heels into the sidewalk and yelled with unladylike ferocity, 'Let go, Willie!'

'Trouble here, Ashley?'

Several people were eyeing them curiously. The man who had spoken had planted himself in front of them. He was a burly, soft-spoken farmer named Jack Yates from the little community of West Hampton, whom Ashley had met at the grocery store on a couple of occasions. 'Willie seems to think I should go for a drive with him,' she said tightly. 'I don't want to, Jack.'

Although Jack was the shorter of the two men, and the older by four or five years, it was local knowledge that he had been an amateur boxer before cattle farming and a pretty girl from nearby Salisbury had caused him to settle down. Now he balanced lightly on the balls of his feet and said calmly, 'Let go of her, Willie.'

'You after her, too, Jack? What does your wife think of that?' Willie sneered. 'One thing about Ashley, she's always available.'

'You hear me?' Jack's voice had dropped. His fists were clenched at his sides.

For a moment it hung on the balance; Ashley could almost feel Willie's indecision through the pores of her skin. He did not want a fight. He wanted her, and he had missed his opportunity. But he would hate to back down from a challenge.

Finally, with a semblance of casualness, Willie

released her. She moved away, rubbing her arm, hearing him say as he walked over to his truck, 'If you want to protect some girl's virtue, Jack, you shouldn't start with Ashley. Because you're too late.'

More humiliated than she had ever been in her life, Ashley felt colour scorch her cheeks. For the first time Jack raised his voice. 'Don't pay any attention to him, Ashley. The people around here know you're not like that.'

'Do they, Jack?' It was an unconscious plea for reassurance.

'Sure they do. You've been here long enough now that people know you're hardworking and honest and doing your best for your family.' From a few remaining onlookers there were murmurs of assent.

Ashley smiled tremulously. 'Thanks, Jack.' If Emma Darby were there, she would not agree. But then Emma would not have approved of the Lord Himself.

Jack had had his say. 'I'll drive you home.'

Ashley accepted his offer, thanked him again when he deposited her in front of the garage, and went to the house to change back into her work clothes. She described the incident to Matthew, knowing he would hear about it via the village grapevine sooner or later, but making as little of it as she could. Then, feeling very tired, she went back to work.

As Saturday evening progressed, Ashley was not sure whether Michael had come to visit herself, or Victoria and Matthew. It did not seem to matter. He fitted into the family as if he had known them for months, getting into long, involved discussions with Matthew and playing with Victoria ... *as a father might*, Ashley thought painfully. She had invited him for dinner, serving roast beef with all the trimmings and a deliciously fluffy rum pie. Now she was brewing the coffee and getting out the cups and saucers while Matthew discoursed on the iniquities of the Income Tax Act to Michael, who was lying flat on his back on the carpet bouncing Victoria on his chest. Michael was groaning in mock agony; Victoria was shrieking with glee. As she lunged for his face, poking at his eyes, he lifted her high above his head and held her there. She gurgled a string of gibberish, punctuating it with a fat, wet bubble. Hastily Michael sat her down again, reaching in his trouser pocket for a handkerchief. 'Revolting child,' he grumbled affectionately.

Ashley turned away, finding the coffee spoons in the drawer. To see Michael's hands holding the body of her child and to listen to their mutual delight in each other filled her with a helpless yearning. Victoria needed someone like Michael. Like every child she had a right to a loving father.

Someone like Michael ... who was she trying to fool? Ashley wondered. She didn't mean that. She meant Michael himself.

Matthew peered over her shoulder, making her jump. 'Have I got time to bring up a load of wood?'

'I'll get it,' offered Michael, putting Victoria down.

'I'm perfectly capable of carrying an armful of logs,' Matthew bristled.

'Thank you, Michael,' Ashley hinted to her grand-father.

'Nag, nag, nag,' complained Matthew, opening the basement door and thudding down the steps.

The coffee was still percolating. Ashley watched its miniature, noisy eruptions, her mind very far away. A father for Victoria ... dimly—and mistakenly—she decided that the intensity of her longing was because she wanted something for Victoria, not for herself.

A hand came to rest on each of her shoulders. 'Penny for them,' Michael offered.

She bent her head. 'They're ten-dollar thoughts.'

With diabolically bad timing, the telephone rang. Michael must have felt the tremor that rippled through her body, and had to have seen how her head swung round to stare at the instrument on the wall as if it were a manifestation of the devil.

Matthew was still in the basement. She had to answer it, Ashley thought sickly; if she didn't, Michael would want to know why. Her feet as heavy as if she was wearing her workboots rather than high-heeled shoes, she walked across the room and picked up the telephone. Her voice a thin thread, she said, 'Hello?'

There was a gloating triumph in the voice at the other end, for once again the hunter had cornered his quarry. Words poured like acid from the man's mouth, vitriolic and soul-destroying words that had a horrible, perverted intimacy. Her face ashen, Ashley replaced the receiver. But the words still rang in her brain. She would remember them for ever . . . she would never feel clean again.

Simultaneously two things happened. Matthew puffed his way up the stairs and Michael crossed the room to take her in his arms. Because she felt smothered in filth, she could not bear the contact. She struck him away.

'Who was it?' Michael demanded. 'Tell me!'

'I don't know,' she cried. 'I don't know his name.'

'So it was anonymous . . . and by the look of you, obscene. It wasn't the first one, was it, Ashley? As soon as the telephone rang, you were afraid, I know you were.'

It was Michael the policeman speaking, the interrogator who would get the truth from her at any cost. 'No, it wasn't the first.'

'Do you have any idea who it is? Not your friend Willie, I wouldn't think—his tactics would be much more direct.'

She had already come to that conclusion. 'No. I'd recognise his voice.'

His eyes fastened on her pale face, Michael said pitilessly, 'But it was Willie who hurt your wrist, wasn't it? And your cheek? That was nothing to do with Victoria.'

At last he got a reaction. Furious with him, Ashley cried, 'Do be quiet!'

But she was too late. Matthew dumped the logs in the woodbox by the stove and said roughly, 'You never told me Willie was around here, Ashley. When? What did he do to you?'

She said meaningfully, 'You know Willie, Grandad, he thinks he's God's gift to women. He got a little rough, that's all.' Her eyes carried a different message. *Careful*, they said. *Michael mustn't find out about Wayne. Don't you dare tell him.*

For once Matthew heeded her. 'That no-good bully!' he blustered. 'He'd better not try any of his tricks when I'm around.' Not at all by accident, his eyes wandered to the shotgun resting on its rack.

Momentarily forgetting Michael, Ashley ordered, 'You'll leave that where it is.'

'And let you be raped in front of my eyes?'

She said impatiently, 'I'm not going to get raped, Grandad.'

Michael cut across their argument, his voice like a whiplash. 'Can you guarantee that?'

She scowled at him. 'Of course not. Any more than I can guarantee that the sun will rise tomorrow morning. But I'm pretty sure it will.'

'You're playing with words, Ashley. None of which will do you any good if you're proved wrong. Willie's mean enough to rape you, don't you fool yourself. He's also smart enough to know that rape could lead to a prison sentence. But I wouldn't count on that deterring him.'

'So what do you suggest I do?' she said sarcastically. 'Move to Halifax and open a hat shop?'

'I'll get you a guard dog.'

'I *beg* your pardon?'

'An old friend of mine near Digby raises trained guard dogs. I'll get you one.'

It was the perfect solution to far more than the problem of Willie, although Michael was not to know that. Ashley said frostily, 'If you do, we'll pay for it.'

Michael said blandly, 'I wasn't suggesting otherwise.

I'll give my friend a call first thing tomorrow morning. With a bit of luck you should have the dog within a week.'

A pleased smile spread across Matthew's face. 'Well, now . . . I've read about those dogs, and I always had a hankering for one. Adds a touch of class to a place.'

Breathing a little easier, Ashley began to pour the coffee. Michael suspected nothing other than Willie's lecherous intents, while Matthew, intrigued by the possibility of owning a guard dog, had the look of Victoria when presented with a new toy. Obviously Wayne McEvoy was not on his mind; there was no risk that he would let anything slip. The crisis was averted.

As it happened, the dog was delivered on Monday. He was a black and tan Alsatian named Toby, with an aristocratic profile and golden, intelligent eyes. He was accompanied by his trainer, Don Berrigan, a short, shy man whose natural diffidence disappeared as he took Toby through his paces and made sure that Matthew and Ashley understood the various words of command. Don spent the better part of the day with them; when he left, Toby settled down as calmly in his new abode as if it had always been home. The dog was never to be effusively friendly, but he did his job without fuss and was an immense comfort to Ashley. Willie no longer seemed such a menace, and even the phone calls were not quite as upsetting.

She knew that Willie had taken note of Toby's presence. Two or three days after Toby arrived, she heard the dog barking. Toby did not bark for the arrival of ordinary customers, so she went to the garage door to investigate. Willie was standing outside. He had obviously tried to walk in through the office door; just as obviously Toby had prevented him. She saw Willie kick out at the dog, who responded with a snarl, lips drawn back to show an array of efficient-looking teeth. She opened the door.

'Can I help you, Willie?' she said politely.

Willie was just about snarling himself. 'Think you're pretty clever, eh?'

'The dog earns his keep,' she responded briefly. 'Did you want something?'

'Nothing that won't wait.' He wheeled, marched back to his truck, and drove off with an aggressive squeal of tyres. And he did not reappear.

The autumn days passed one by one, and with each one the coming of winter seemed a little more inevitable. The last of the maples' scarlet leaves had drifted earthward, while the birches lifted a tangle of black branches to the sky; only the beech trees rustled and shook with their dry bronze foliage. By the time Ashley closed the garage at suppertime, it was dark; and it was dark when she got up in the mornings, often to find the gas pumps and garage windows rimed with frost. The deer season opened, the autumn winds carrying the reverberation of rifle shots from deep in the woods. Some of these shots found their mark, for cars and trucks drove past the garage with carcasses sprawled across them, a sight that always made Ashley cringe.

Normally it was not a time of year she liked. But this year seemed different, the days carrying the sharp bright promise of spring rather than the sombre decay of November. She would not even admit to herself that the change was due to Michael, and certainly would not have admitted it to Matthew.

For Michael had become a regular part of her life. Sometimes she visited him at Valleyview Farm, although more often he drove to Lower Hampton. After Victoria was in bed, the three of them would sit around the kitchen table, playing cards, laughing and talking: a modern version of the Three Musketeers, Ashley sometimes thought with an inward smile. She was beginning to wonder if she had imagined Michael telling her he was falling in love with her, for he gave no signs of being a man in love now. His manner towards her was warm and friendly; but then so was his manner to Matthew. He showed more open affection to Victoria than he did to Victoria's mother. At first Ashley was glad of this, for of course she was not in love with him and she would not want him hurt. But as she grew to know him better and to like what she saw more and more, she found herself wishing he would take her in his arms again with that look of tenderness in his face; that he would kiss her as if she was the only woman in the world; that he would stroke her hair as if its beauty had mesmerised him. He did none of these things. He was, she thought irritably, the perfect gentleman. And she, who should have appreciated that, did not.

There was another factor in their relationship: Tim, the belligerent redhead who liked to run away. Several days after Ashley's first meeting with Tim, Michael brought the boy over for the afternoon, leaving him and Ashley together in the garage. 'Hello, Tim,' said Ashley. 'How are you today?'

'Fine.'

She gave him a friendly smile, which he did not return. 'I'm glad you're wearing old clothes ... were you able to get the tiller started?'

'Yeah. I ran it like you said. And cleaned the sponge.'

That was a long speech for Tim. He was standing with his shoulders hunched and his hands thrust in his pockets, waiting for her next move. She sensed there was no point in trying to woo him with overtures of friendliness or with personal questions; the former he would resent and the latter ignore. So she said calmly, 'Okay, I've got to fix a flat, and then do a grease job. Feel free to ask questions, that's the way to learn.'

She showed him each step for changing the flat tire, letting him work the air wrench to remove the bolts and showing him how to locate and plug the leak. Then she painstakingly took him through the whole procedure of the oil change, running the car over the pit so both she and Tim could get underneath as she removed the drain plug and oil filter. She greased the tie rod ends, idler

arm, drag link, and ball joints, then climbed up the
narrow little stairs to lift the hood and begin a whole
series of checks there. She explained everything she was
doing, and whenever possible let Tim do some of the
work himself.

She could not have faulted his attention; she didn't
think he missed a single word that she said. Although at
first he observed in silence, his curiosity soon got the
better of him, and the questions started. Ashley
answered each one as best she could, being careful not
to smile at those which betrayed his ignorance. A
couple of times she showed him how to look things up
in the automotive manuals; she always named each tool
that she used and described its function; she slipped in
the occasional question herself to test his knowledge.
Midway through the afternoon, as they were checking
the air pressure in the tyres and looking for signs of
wear, she risked asking, 'Do you like living at
Valleyview?'

He shot her an inimical look. 'It's okay. Why do the
tires have to be cold?'

Wrong move, Ashley . . . She dredged up her high
school physics to answer his question and did not make
the same mistake again. But it was not easy to hold
back her natural feelings. As Tim leaned over the fender
to peer at the water level in the battery, she saw how his
vivid hair curled against the narrow nape of his neck—
which could have done with washing. The veins in his
wrists were blue under the skin, and he was far too thin.
She wanted to take him into her arms and hold him
tight, to protect him from any more pain. She wanted
to tell him that it was all right to trust and to love, and
that running away solved nothing.

Yet Michael had accused her of running away; and
she had as much as admitted that because of David
she was frightened to trust a man again, or to allow
herself to fall in love. So, apart from being a little
more adept at hiding her feelings, how was she
different from Tim? How could she possibly fault Tim

for an attitude that she herself had espoused ... with far less cause.

When Michael came to get Tim to take him back to the farm, she looked the boy straight in the eye and said evenly, 'You're welcome to come here any time you can, Tim.'

Those heartbreakingly thick lashes dropped down to mask the grey eyes. The boy shuffled his feet. 'Thanks,' he muttered.

A small word, but something of a victory. Ashley added prosaically, 'See that container on the wall? It's hand cleaner—squirt some on and rub it in and then rinse under the hose. It should get the worst of the grease off.'

As the boy did as he was told, she said to Michael, loudly enough that Tim would hear, 'I hope you'll bring him again.'

'I will. How's Toby working out?'

'Fine. Willie got the message.'

'Good. Hurry up, Tim, we've got to go.'

Michael was leaning against the doorway, looking very much at ease, his blue eyes wandering around the garage. He was paying her no attention whatsoever. She stood her ground, feeling as if some of Tim's truculence had rubbed off on her. 'Have I done something to offend you?' she asked in the same even voice with which she had addressed Tim.

His eyes flew to her face. 'Heavens, no. Why?'

Wishing the question unsaid, she mumbled, 'Oh, I don't know. I just wondered.'

'Of course not. You must know how much I enjoy your company.'

And Matthew's company and Victoria's company ... She gave him a false smile. 'Well, I'd better get back to work. Goodbye, Tim.' She reached for a spanner and bent over the engine of the car, hoping her back view looked sufficiently industrious and uncaring, for her eyes were blurred with tears. She heard them leave via the office door, heard—how could she help it?—the assorted roars, rattles and squeals as the jeep got underway, and out of the corner of her eye watched it drive away. Only then did she put down the spanner.

Maybe he's in love with someone else.

Come off it, Ashley, you don't believe that.

He's not in love with me.

Well, that's a little more likely.

He doesn't want a woman who's a fighter—even though that was his own word. He doesn't want a woman who's not a virgin, and who's got a child.

That's not what he said.

That's what he's saying now.

You could be right.

Argument over. Ashley slumped against the car door, all the old uncertainties and fears overwhelming her, just as, outside, the dark-edged November clouds had hidden the sun. *Why do I care so much? Why does it matter to me?* They were two questions she was unable to answer. And as Michael's friendly, innocuous visits continued, she found herself less and less able to answer them.

Tim came twice more. The second visit was very much the same as the first, Ashley demonstrating some of the basic techniques of automobile maintenance and refraining from any overt moves of friendship. But on Tim's third visit she allowed him to do more of the work, although always under her supervision. He worked neatly and quickly, with an instinctive feel for the tools and the engine parts that could not be learned from any manual. He was trying very hard to be nonchalant about his newly learned skills; but as he finished replacing a fan-belt, she saw the glow of pride in the grey eyes. She said, smiling, 'You did a good job, Tim.'

He turned away to replace the tools he had been using, mumbling an indeterminate reply.

She felt a flicker of anger and said deliberately, 'The appropriate response when someone compliments you is to say thank you.'

He avoided her eyes. 'Oh. Thanks.'

'My name is Ashley.'

He said with seeming irrelevance, 'I gotta call the housekeeper *Mrs* Collins.'

'As I'm not married, you can't very well call me Mrs MacCulloch. Ashley will do just fine.'

'Ashley's a boy's name.'

'It can be a girl's name, too.'

He was restlessly shifting his feet, but she was determined to hold her ground. She repeated gravely, 'You did a good job, Tim.'

He blushed and muttered, 'Thank you, Ashley.'

She quickly squeezed his shoulder, feeling the bird-like bones under his shirt, and releasing him before he could move away. 'I'll park this car outside and bring in the Ford. We have to replace the alternator.' Her voice, she hoped, was matter-of-fact; her feelings were not. As she had clasped the thin shoulder, knowing he was resenting her touch, she had felt an overwhelming rush of tenderness, combined with a fierce longing to give him the permanence and love that he needed. *Don't be crazy, Ashley*, she scolded herself as she backed the car outdoors. *You're old enough to know you can't cure all the ills of the world. Besides, Tim's getting the best of care at Valleyview.* All of which was no doubt reasonable and true, even if it did not seem to help much.

She was confused about Tim; she was more than confused about Michael; the only bright spot seemed to be that Wayne—and Willie—were leaving her alone. The phone calls had ceased and Willie's red truck stayed out of the yard. Ashley could only assume that Wayne had given up, belatedly having concluded that Matthew could neither be bought nor intimidated. She discovered there could be another reason a couple of days after Tim's visit when she was chatting idly to Donnie Yates, a cousin of Jack's, while she replaced the battery in his truck. 'Too bad about the park, eh?' said Donnie.

'Park? What park?'

'Haven't you heard the rumours that they might be opening up a new National Park five miles from here? In the Trout Lake area.'

'I did hear something to that effect a few weeks ago. I didn't pay much attention.'

'They say now it's been scrapped. Would have brought a fair bit of employment to the area, as well as all those tourist dollars. Too bad.'

Ashley gaped at him, her brain instantly making the connection. Wayne had heard the rumours about the park. That was why he had wanted to buy the garage, which as the only gasoline outlet in the immediate area represented a potential goldmine; Wayne would be quick to realise that. But now, apparently, there was to be no development. It could not be coincidence that Wayne's attempt to frighten Matthew into selling the garage had also ceased.

Feeling as though a load had been lifted from her shoulders, Ashley said insincerely, 'It is a pity, yes.' At lunchtime she hurried over to the house and shared the good news with Matthew, after which they danced a little jig around the kitchen, much to Victoria's edification.

In a way, now that it was over, Ashley wanted to share the whole ugly story with Michael. But a streak of caution kept her silent; that, and the knowledge that indirectly she had lied to him. Nevertheless, she should have been in good humour when he dropped in that evening. She was wearing a new burgundy-red pullover with tailored grey slacks, her hair braided in a coronet, and knew she looked her best; it irked her when his glance slid over her casually. It annoyed her even more when he made a tremendous fuss of Victoria and then, after the child had gone to bed, settled down to a game of chess with Matthew.

She tucked herself in the corner with a book, purposely withdrawing from them. But the pages failed to hold her attention. She found herself watching the faint frown on Michael's forehead as he planned his strategy, and the way his long, lean fingers picked up the ivory pieces, absently caressing them. Then, furious with herself, she would force her eyes back to the page. By eleven o'clock, with the game showing no signs of coming to an end, she was thoroughly out of sorts. She yawned elaborately, closing the book. 'I'm going to bed,' she announced.

Matthew, whose bishop was courting disaster, grunted a good night. Michael smiled at her and said amiably, 'Your turn to come my way, Ashley. How about Wednesday evening?'

Don't take me for granted, Michael Gault, she thought angrily. 'I wasn't aware we were taking turns,' she said, carefully inserting the bookmark between two pages that she had not yet read. 'Thank you, but I'd rather not.'

Ostentatiously Matthew pushed back his chair. 'Guess I'll get a load of wood.'

'Grandad, the wood box is full!'

'Then I might as well go to the bathroom while I'm up.'

'There's no need to be so tactful!' Ashley fumed. 'I'm going to bed, anyway.'

Matthew said shrewdly, 'You look like you're itching for a fight, girl,' and ambled off in the direction of the bathroom, his mustard-yellow sweater drooping from his shoulders.

Ashley got up, too. 'Good night, Michael.'

He was too quick for her. Getting to his feet, he blocked off her exit to the hall. 'What's wrong with Wednesday?'

She wanted her exit to be cool and disdainful; she should have said in a very dignified manner, 'I have other plans.' Instead she spat, 'Shall I bring Matthew and Victoria?'

'So that's the problem ... They're part of your family, Ashley. I enjoy being with them.'

'Good. Then you come here on Wednesday, and I'll make sure I'm out.'

'You do want a fight, don't you?'

She had always known he could move fast. But now she found herself locked in his embrace and being comprehensively kissed before she could draw a breath of protest. His hands were digging into her ribs, pulling her against the hard wall of his chest. There was no tenderness in his kiss, no searching for her response; it was instead a kiss of mastery and domination. She fought against it, filled with an impotent fury, wriggling, kicking, her fingers curved into claws. But under his onslaught her lips parted, his tongue touching hers; so suddenly that she staggered, one arm loosened its hold and his fingers cupped her breast.

Like fire leaping from treetop to treetop, her need of him streaked along her veins, consuming reason and inhibition in a white blaze of passion. She clasped his shoulders, moulding the bone and muscle, feeling her nipples tighten and her body melt. Her last coherent thought was that maybe, just maybe, the poets *were* right . . .

Matthew contrived to slam the bathroom door and clomped back along the passage to the kitchen. In no great hurry Michael drew back from her, his eyes as primitive with passion as her own must be. For her ears alone he murmured, 'I think you should leave Matthew and Victoria at home on Wednesday.'

She was breathing as rapidly as if she had been running. 'I haven't said I'll come.'

'Please, Ashley.'

She saw the wicked sparkle in his eyes. She also saw the brilliance of desire. But before she could answer, Matthew said plaintively, 'It's your move, Michael.'

'No, it's Ashley's move. Ashley?'

'Yes,' she whispered. 'Yes, I'll come.'

He kissed her without haste. 'I'll look forward to seeing you. Good night . . . sleep well.'

It was no accident that his arm brushed her breast. She said shakily, not daring to meet his gaze, 'Good night. 'Night, Grandad,' and fled from the room.

CHAPTER SEVEN

THE next morning when Ashley came downstairs with Victoria in her arms, Matthew was in his usual pose by the stove stirring the porridge. He grunted a greeting, doled out the porridge and said, 'You know he's in love with you, don't you?'

A number of replies hovered on Ashley's tongue. Perversely she replied, 'Who's in love with me, Grandad? Up you go, Vickie love.' She hoisted the baby into her high-chair.

'You know darn well who I mean. And being the kind of man he is, he'll ask you to marry him.'

'I presume you're talking about Michael.'

'Of course I am! Who else?'

'Just as long as it's not Willie,' she said naughtily.

Matthew slammed the sugar bowl down on the table. 'Will you please be serious for a minute?'

She glared across the table into his fiery old eyes. 'Very well. I am not in love with Michael, and if he asks me to marry him, which I should think is highly unlikely, I shall say no. Is that what you wanted to know?'

'Then you're a damn fool!'

Ashley stirred Victoria's cereal with unnecessary vigour. 'I really would prefer to begin the day without having an argument, Grandad.'

She might as well have saved her breath. 'What have you got against him?' snorted Matthew. 'He's good-looking, he's got money, he's intelligent, and he plays a darn good game of chess. What more do you want?'

'Maybe I don't want to marry anyone—even such a paragon of virtue as Michael Gault,' she responded with regrettable sarcasm.

'Sure you do. The two of you are made for each

other. And he loves Victoria.' Matthew sat back with a self-satisfied smile, obviously certain that he had clinched his case.

'Then let him wait twenty years and marry Victoria.'

'It's you he wants to marry, Ashley.'

'Did he tell you that?'

'No need. I've got eyes—I saw the two of you last night.'

Ashley shovelled some cereal into Victoria's open mouth, willing herself not to blush. 'Grandad, you've been around long enough to know there's a three-letter word called sex. It does not necessarily bear any relationship to either love or marriage.'

'With men like Michael Gault, it does. Just because you picked one bad apple it doesn't mean the whole barrel is rotten.'

'Maybe I've decided I don't like apples.'

'Stuff and nonsense!'

As if she agreed, Victoria gave one of her juiciest belches. Ashley smothered a smile and said more mildly, 'Grandad, Michael has never said he loves me and has certainly never asked me to marry him. I promise you'll be the first one to know if he does. But just don't hold your breath until it happens, okay? Because, cantankerous as you are, I like having you around.'

'Oh, I'll still be around when he asks you. And I won't be much older, either. One or two pieces of toast?'

As usual, Matthew had managed to have the last word. Nor could Ashley easily dismiss what he had said, because Matthew at times showed an uncanny prescience, and far too many of his forecasts had been proved right for her present peace of mind. She would have been edgy enough about her proposed visit to Valleyview on Wednesday evening after Michael's devastating kiss in the kitchen; with Matthew's predictions hovering in her brain, she was doubly nervous. Nothing in her wardrobe seemed suitable, for she found herself with a strong aversion to dressing in any way that could be interpreted as seductive. In the end she put on a pair of jeans and a cable-knit sweater over a white blouse, gathering her hair into a knot at the nape of her neck. Nothing seductive about that, she thought, regarding herself in the mirror with satisfaction. What she did not see was how the boyish cut of the clothes subtly emphasised her femininity: the slender legs, narrow waist, and firm young breasts. Nor was she aware of how gracefully she moved, which had nothing to do with what she was wearing.

Reassured that she could not possibly cause Michael to lose his head, she ran downstairs. Matthew regarded her without any great enthusiasm. 'No need to hurry home now that we've got Toby.'

'I won't be very late,' she replied. 'Working day tomorrow.' She put on a windproof jacket and boots, for the temperature had dropped, and added mischievously, 'I bet you a dollar my marital status won't even be discussed this evening.'

'Done. Although if you're that sure, you should make it ten dollars.'

'I'll make it twenty,' she said airily. Which, she was to think afterwards, went to show how abysmally wrong she could be.

It was a horrible night, November at its worst. The wind keened through the bare-limbed trees and tugged at her jacket, the bite of winter in its clinging fingers. The ground was frozen and the puddles skimmed with ice, while the sky was an unrelieved and depthless black, the stars obscured by low-hanging clouds.

Toby sniffed at her boots and Ashley patted him on the head. He deigned to wag his tail, watching her as she got in the Honda and started it up. As her headlights disappeared round the corner, he wandered back to his kennel on the sheltered side of the garage.

Ashley enjoyed her journeys to Valleyview. Her life was such that she was rarely alone, so it made a pleasant change to drive through the darkness all by herself, able to think her own thoughts without interruption. She had met all the residents of Valleyview by now, and several of the boys had become distinct personalities to her, although it was still Tim with whom she felt the closest tie. Michael might say that he was accomplishing no miracles at Valleyview; she herself could only admire what he was doing. Day in and day out he was there: solid, real, and caring. Yet he was no wishy-washy do-gooder, for he had principles and stuck by them regardless of whether they made him popular or not. She could not help contrasting him with her father, to the detriment of the latter. Her father had substituted rules for love, whereas Michael's rules—far fewer—were dictated by his love and concern for the boys in his charge.

She now knew about the sizeable fortune Michael had inherited from his father, and of the mental discomfort it had caused him. His father sounded to Ashley like an urban version of Wayne McEvoy, a big-city businessman not overly particular about the way he had amassed his fortune. His son must be his direct opposite. 'Born with a social conscience,' Michael had admitted with a disparaging grin. Ashley knew it was not as simple as that, and respected Michael for the choices he had made. He could have lived a life of leisure had he chosen to do so, drifting from continent to continent in a hedonistic search for entertainment. Instead he had exposed himself for years to the dangers and frustrations of an undercover agent, and now was involved in the often thankless task of re-channelling young lives that had gone wrong. He was a very different man from David. In an unwary moment near the end of their relationship David had as much as admitted to her that he wanted to be a doctor for the money and the prestige, not from any altruistic desire to aid suffering humanity. It had shocked her at the time, that admission, for it had opened another crack in the once flawless love she had given him. Now she was more able to realise that David's rewards would be only as great as his contribution. David would never understand Michael's frustrations and never experience his joy; not for him those depths and heights. David would be paid in the same coin he tendered.

None of which meant that she loved Michael . . . did it? And there Ashley's thoughts came to a full stop.

Wisp-like threads of snow were being driven towards the headlights, the first snow of the season. *If it snows I won't be able to stay long,* she thought. *Probably just as well. Because what I really want is for this relationship between me and Michael to stay exactly as it is. Companionship. Fun. An attractive escort when I need one. But nothing more. No decisions. No talk of love and marriage.* She smiled to herself. *And I'll use Matthew's twenty dollars to buy a new blouse.*

She turned off the highway and drove along the lane beside the stream, where the rocks each had a brittle halo of ice and the moss was frozen to the ground. As she reached the top of the hill her eyes widened in surprise, for every window in the house was a blaze of light, from the basement to the attic.

She parked the car and ran to Michael's door, rapping sharply on the panels. No answer. Waiting a few seconds, she banged the brass knocker, but again there was no response. For a moment she stayed where she was, as frozen to the doorstep as the fragile mosses were to their rocks and boulders. Why wasn't Michael home? Had something happened to him? Was he ill . . . or had he been hurt? Brian, the oldest of the boys at Valleyview, had a history of violence and aggression. What if Brian had attacked him?

She stumbled round to the front of the house. The door was unlocked. Opening it, she stepped inside.

The hall with its oak banisters and polished floors was just as usual. Bright yellow chrysanthemums in a pewter bowl stood stiffly on the mahogany table. Jackets and running shoes were jammed into the closet. Rock music echoed from another part of the house.

Ashley could hear her own heartbeat, a steady thud

as insistent as the thump of the bass from the unseen stereo. She started off across the hall in that direction. Then she stopped, calling out, 'Is anyone there?'

Footsteps were approaching from the kitchen area. Heavy, no-nonsense footsteps. Mrs Collins, the house-keeper, put her head around the door. 'Oh, it's you, dear. I thought it might be someone with some news.'

'What's happened?' *Not Michael . . . please God, not Michael.*

'Tim's run away again, the young scalawag. Mr Gault's fit to be tied.' Mrs Collins with her stout form and tight grey curls belonged to the old school where the boss was the boss and as such was given his proper title. Everyone else was indiscriminately, 'dear'. 'He's checking the sheds, I believe. Trouble is, there's only the two of us here right now. Mr Parker's not due back for a couple of hours.' Mr Parker was the teacher Michael employed on a full-time basis. 'Maybe you should go and find Mr Gault. I'm sure he'd be glad of your help.'

Ashley gave Mrs Collins a quick smile. 'All right, I'll do that.' *He's safe . . . thank heavens he's safe!*

As she ran across the front yard towards the sheds, she saw a light flick on in the building where she had first seen Tim surrounded by the entrails of the tiller. Michael was safe; but Tim was not. The wind moaned around the corner of the house, the thick impenetrable darkness vanquishing the glow of light from the shed window, and she felt fear catch at her heart again. Surely Tim wasn't out in this. He must be hiding somewhere in the house or in one of the barns; he couldn't be alone in the icy, windswept night.

Michael came out of the shed. He was alone, and even across the distance that separated them she could tell from his demeanour that Tim had not been found. Her boots crunching in the gravelled walk, she ran towards him, and as she did so it was as if she saw him for the first time. He was silhouetted against the light, his face turned towards the bleak emptiness of the meadows that stretched to the unseen river. Michael, with his penetrating blue eyes and his injured body; Michael, who was not afraid to care for others and who put his caring into concrete action; Michael, whose ready wit camouflaged a courage and an intensity that called to her own spirit, giving it wings to fly towards him ... Through the darkness she cried his name, and saw him turn and stare in her direction, blinded by the light from the shed.

She closed the distance between them and flung her arms around him, her voice muffled in his jacket. 'I was afraid when I saw all the lights that something had happened to you. I'm so glad you're safe. But Tim— you haven't found him?'

By reflex Michael's arms had gone around her. As she looked up, she saw new lines graven in his cheeks and had her answer before he spoke. 'No. No sign of him anywhere in the house or around the outbuildings. I think he's headed for the woods.'

'Alone?'

'Yes. He's a loner, anyway. Hasn't made any close friends here.'

'Wouldn't he go towards the road and try to hitch a ride?'

'Not Tim. He's not running towards anything or anywhere, Ashley, that's not the object. He's running away—literally.'

'From *what*?'

Michael ran his fingers through his hair. 'I wish I knew. One of the older boys—Kevin, remember him?— left here today to live in a foster-home and go to high school in Halifax—a good move for him. But Tim probably interpreted it as yet another demonstration of impermanence. I blame myself for not taking the time to explain to him why Kevin was leaving, I should have known what would happen. Just when he was starting to show a few signs of trust, too. Now we'll be right back where we started.'

'What are we going to *do*?' The 'we' slipped out without her even noticing it.

'You're going to stay in the house. I'm going down by the river. I have a hunch I know where he'll be.'

'I'm coming with you.'

'Ashley, don't be——'

She said unequivocally, 'I care about him too, Michael.'

Michael gave her a level stare that seemed to see into her very soul. 'Okay. We'll go up to the house and get some extra clothing for him and a couple of flashlights. And we'll tell Beth Collins if we're not back in an hour to call the police. Because if Tim's not where I think he is, we're in bad trouble. Let's go.'

Only a few minutes later they were leaving the house together, Ashley's flashlight cutting a yellow swathe in the darkness, Michael with a haversack on his back containing some of Tim's clothes and a thermos of hot tea. He had loaned Ashley a hat, which she pulled down snugly over her ears to protect them from the wind, glad she had worn her jeans and sweater even if for all the wrong reasons; glad, too, that the snow seemed to have stopped. To try and banish the nightmare vision of Tim's skinny little body huddled against the cold, she said, 'Where do you think he'll be?'

'One of two places. To the north along the riverbank some of the boys have built a camp out of old lumber—he could be there. I hope so, it'll shelter him from the wind. Or in the opposite direction there are a couple of caverns among the rocks on the bank, he was very interested in them on one of our treks. I just hope to God he hasn't gone wandering off into the woods.'

So did she. Trying to be practical, she suggested, 'Why don't we separate when we get to the river? You go one way and I'll go the other. It would save time.'

They were crossing the expanse of the meadow, Ashley occasionally tripping over tussocks of grass, for the slope was steep. Although she shrank from the thought of being alone in the woods at night, her fear was overcome by a sense of urgency: Tim must be found, and soon.

Michael said slowly, 'It would be safer to stay together. I don't want you getting lost, too.'

'I'll promise not to leave the riverbank—that way I can't get lost. It's so cold, Michael—time could be all-important.' In spite of herself, her voice shook.

'Yeah . . .' He made the decision. 'It would be better if you headed for the caves, the terrain isn't as difficult that way and it's not as far. They're unmistakable because there's a cliff face that comes almost to the water's edge, and the caves are on the west face. Two of them, very pretty in summer, because they're overhung with ferns, and trout lilies bloom all around them. Not so pretty now, I'm afraid.'

'If he's not there, will I come back the same way?'

'Right. I'll mark the meeting place. You may have to wait for a while because it'll take me longer to get to the treehouse.'

Ashley did not dare say anything about Michael's injured knee, for she knew he had forgotten about it totally. 'Maybe you should give me a sweater in case I find him.'

They had reached the edge of the woods. 'I'll do that. Okay, we'd better go single file now. There's a trail through the trees, but it's pretty narrow.' From his pocket Michael took a strip of orange plastic and tied it to the nearest branch. 'In case there's any trouble, I'll mark the path as we go.'

Ashley was shivering from more than the cold. She had thought the meadow was dark, yet the forest loomed ahead with a denser blackness than any she had ever known, a primeval blackness as if stars and sun had ceased to exist and eternal night had fallen on the earth. Fitfully, carried on the wind, came the ripple and splash of the river. Keeping her flashlight trained on the ground, she stumbled along at Michael's heels. Sharp-pointed twigs caught at her hat; branches slapped her legs. The icy breath of the wind had found every gap in her clothing, piercing the sturdy denim of her jeans and chilling her fingertips in their wool gloves. She noticed these discomforts with one part of her mind; the other part was preoccupied by Tim's plight, which was probably much worse than her own.

The noise of the river gradually changed from a distant, pleasant murmur to a rowdy, turbulent roaring between its banks. There had been a lot of rain in November. As Michael shone his torch across the water to the far shore, another horrifying vision flashed into Ashley's brain: Tim scrambling along the rocky bank and slipping, falling into the cold, roiling waters and being swept away, his cries for help heard only by the uncaring forest.

As if he had read her mind, Michael said roughly, 'He may only be ten, but he's no fool, Ashley, and he's been looking after himself for a long time.'

She swallowed. 'Which way do I go?'

'Down river. It's only about half a mile as the crow flies, but you'll have to take your time.' His face was very serious in the torchlight. 'Be careful, won't you? Don't stray away from the bank.'

'I won't. You be careful, too.'

He passed her Tim's sweater, which she knotted around her waist under her jacket. Then he lowered his head and kissed her cold lips. 'I know you're frightened—but you'll be all right. And Ashley—I'm glad you're here.'

'I'm glad, too,' she said simply. And strangely enough, despite the cold and the wind and the encroaching violence of the river, she knew she would not want to be anywhere else. 'I'll see you later.'

He was tying another of the plastic strips around the silvery trunk of a birch tree. 'Right here,' he said, raising his hand in salute. 'Good luck.'

Ashley resolutely directed her flashlight downstream and began picking her way along the shore, ducking under the swaying boughs of spruce trees, detouring around impenetrable clumps of alders, the cacophony of the river always in her ears. Every two or three minutes she stopped and yelled Tim's name, swinging the flashlight deeper into the woods that crowded to the water's edge. Of necessity her progress was painfully slow, for there was no path, and the jumble of rocks were slippery with spray from the river. But she was making progress; and inwardly she could only pray that Michael was right in his assessment of Tim's actions, so that the boy would be found in the next hour.

She had been travelling for about ten minutes when she felt the first cold brush of snow against her face. Raising her light, she saw scattered flakes whirling earthward from the black sky. Her heart sank, for coupled with the wind and the darkness it was yet another obstacle to their search. Perhaps it was only a flurry like the last one . . . nothing to be alarmed about.

Her optimism was short-lived. The snowflakes multiplied, swirling about her in a ghostly dance, white wraiths mocking her with beckoning arms and ever-shifting forms.

Keeping her flashlight low, Ashley clambered over the rocks, stubbornly shouting Tim's name into the driven snow. She came to a sharp bend in the river, where a curved beach of grey sand had accumulated on the lee shore, no doubt an idyllic spot in the summer. But now the beach was bare of footprints; grimly she struggled on.

She almost walked into the cliff, so suddenly did it emerge from the blackness, its sheer face masked by stunted trees. Her heartbeat quickened. 'Tim!' she cried. 'Tim—where are you?' Straining her ears, she heard nothing but the tumble of water between the rocks and the whine of the wind.

Very carefully she inched her way along the rock wall, whose ledges were hung with the dry brown skeletons of last summer's ferns. The first cave that Michael had described was a V-shaped fissure between two great slabs of granite, scarcely big enough to hold even a boy as thin as Tim. It was empty. The second was twenty feet further away from the river. Again it was a cleft between two chunks of granite, although deeper than the first. Ashley had always had a horror of small spaces. The narrow black cavern, barely five feet high, was like the setting for her worst nightmares, filled with the sinister presence of someone, or something, waiting for her to enter...

She threw a beam of yellow light into the cave, seeing only more dead bracken and frozen moss, and croaked Tim's name. But he was not there. An untidy pile of rock closed off the back of the cave; he could not possibly have squeezed behind it.

Bitterly disappointed, filled with an intense fear for the safety of the ill-mannered, skinny little redhead she had come to love, Ashley stood irresolutely, the snow whipping around her body. She could only conclude that Tim had not headed this way, that instead he had gone in the opposite direction towards the camp. It would have been a more logical choice, certainly, considering the bitter weather. Michael would find Tim at the camp, she thought stoutly. She'd better head back to their meeting place so she wouldn't cause any delay.

She was never to understand why she made a last-minute sweep of the granite boulders with her torch, nor why she flung Tim's name one more time into the teeth of the wind.

From high above her head, an eerie cry pierced the night. She stood like an ice-statute, the yellow light shining upward, every muscle in her body aching with strain. The wind buffeted the trees. A branch creaked. At her feet the brown fronds rustled. Overriding all the other sounds was the constant roar of the swollen river.

Then she heard it again—a thin, disembodied cry, like that of a wounded bird. For a moment she was terror-stricken, for it seemed as though the wind had spoken, or the wraiths of snow had given voice. Gripping the flashlight, her hand shaking, she defiantly yelled a human name into the air. 'Tim! Tim . . .'

There could be no mistake this time. Her call had been answered. From somewhere ahead of her, and to her right . . . forgetting her promise to Michael that she would not leave the banks of the river, Ashley scrambled another thirty feet along the ledge. 'Tim!' she shouted with all the force of her lungs. 'Tim, where are you?'

Again the cry came from above her head. This time it was tangible, unquestionably the voice of a small boy. 'Up here—here I am!'

Instinctively her hand followed the sound. But all she saw was a twenty-foot wall of granite, the boulders smaller now, thrown in a careless heap by a giant's hand. She lowered the beam of the flashlight, picked out a route over the tumbled rocks and began to climb, her gloved fingers grasping every handhold along the way. She could not hurry, for there were gaping crevices between the rocks, where one slip could mean a broken ankle; and she was hindered by the flashlight, which she was terrified of dropping.

She was panting by the time she reached the top. Shining the torch over the little plateau, she saw Tim immediately. He was cowering in a hollow of sharp-edged rocks, blinking in the light, his red hair and blue jacket powdered with snow. For an instant her whole being was a fervent cry of gratitude.

With exquisite care she slid down one rock, rounded another, stepped over a third. And then she had reached him. She rested the torch in a niche. Putting her arms around him, she gave him a fierce hug, muttering dementedly, 'Oh, Tim, I'm so glad I've found you! I was so worried. I almost didn't hear you, thank God I did. Are you all right?'

He had butted his head into her shoulder; she could feel him shaking, and sensed that he was crying. She held him close, rocking him back and forth, murmuring soothing bits of nonsense into his ear even as, more practically, she tried to shelter his body from the wind.

Eventually he quietened. Only then did she risk looking down into his tear-streaked face. 'I thought you'd be in one of the caves, not up here,' she said.

'I was going to stay in the cave. But I climbed up here first to see what it was like.' His voice quivered. 'I slipped and hurt my ankle—I can't walk. That's why I had to stay here.'

Ashley loosened her hold on him and brought the torch down to shine on his feet. He was wearing running shoes with frayed laces. 'Which one?' she said economically.

'The right one. It hurts.'

Very gently she probed the area around his ankle. Although it was badly swollen, she was not knowledgeable enough to know if it was broken or only sprained. 'You can't rest your weight on it?'

'No. I tried.'

She pushed back a mental image of the pain and fear he must have felt. Brushing the snow from his hair, she took off her hat and pulled it down over his head. 'I don't need it because I can pull up the hood of my jacket,' she explained. 'I've got an extra sweater here, let's take your jacket off and put it on underneath. Then you'll feel warmer.' Once this was accomplished she sat back on her heels, regarding him dubiously. He gave her a wavering smile.

Ashley said carefully, 'You know, we'd be a lot better off if we could get down to one of the caves. They're much more sheltered than it is up here. It could take Michael quite a while to get back to us, you see, because he went the other way—to the camp.' The fear she did not voice was that Michael might not see them up here at all, just as she had so nearly missed finding Tim herself.

'We could try.'

'You hold the torch and shine it ahead of us. I'll take as much of your weight as I can. Ready?' She gave him a smile with all the encouragement in it she could muster.

She got Tim to his feet without too much trouble. But he could not bear to put even a minimum of weight on his sore foot, and slight though he was, he was too heavy for her to lift. They managed two shuffling steps. Then his injured ankle banged against a rock. He screamed, a horrible animal sound of pain that tore along her nerves. Kneeling, Ashley lowered him to the ground, feeling him tremble all over. 'Oh, Tim, I'm sorry,' she stammered. 'We'll have to wait for Michael. I'm just not strong enough to hold you.' Trying to block out the memory of that dreadful scream, she went on, 'Let's at least get as comfortable as we can.'

She settled herself with her back against a ledge and eased Tim up on her lap, putting her arm around him and holding him as closely as she could. The flashlight she balanced so that the beam went skyward; it was the only thing she could do to attract Michael's attention. 'Are you okay?' she murmured to Tim. 'You're not too cold, are you?' As he shook his head, she added in sudden inspiration, 'Hey, I nearly forgot—Michael gave me a couple of chocolate bars. Let's eat them.'

They were in her jacket pocket. Her fingers numb with cold, Ashley managed to unwrap them, and for a few minutes she and Tim ate in silence. Chocolate had never tasted so good; Ashley savoured each mouthful, trying to make the bar last as long as she could. When she had finished, she shoved the wrapper in her pocket. 'I could eat two or three more of those,' she said regretfully.

'Me, too.' There was a silence. Then Tim added in a small voice, 'Thank you, Ashley.'

She squeezed his shoulders, remembering his initial reluctance to call her by name. 'You're welcome. Tim, why did you run away?'

Another silence, longer this time. Ashley waited. He could not in any physical sense run from her question, but he could, of course, refuse to answer it, retreating into the moodiness and defiance that seemed to characterise his dealings with adults. Whatever the result, she did not regret asking the question, for she had earned the right to do so over the past couple of hours.

'They took Kevin away today,' Tim said finally.

'Yes, that's right. He went to a foster-home in Halifax so he could go to high school.'

'I don't want to do that!'

'You don't have to, Tim. For Kevin it was the right thing at this particular time. For you it probably wouldn't be.'

'I want to stay at the farm.'

You have a funny way of showing it . . . But she did not say this. 'Have you told Mr Gault that you'd like to stay?'

'No.'

'Maybe he doesn't realise that you want to stay. Maybe he thinks because you keep running away, you hate it at Valleyview.'

'I don't hate it!'

'Tell him that, then, Tim.'

'I figured he'd know.'

'Just because he's an adult, he's not necessarily a mind-reader. I can't speak for him, Tim, but I'm almost sure he'd really like you to stay at Valleyview. But you can't keep on doing this sort of thing. It's dangerous for you, and for other people, too.'

Another long silence. The wind seemed to have dropped a little. A snowflake drifted on to Tim's hat, and Ashley stared at it absorbedly, fascinated by the geometric elegance of something intrinsically so short-lived. Then Tim burst out, 'You've got a baby—you didn't give it away. Not like my mother.'

They had come to the crux of the matter. 'No, I didn't, Tim. But I was lucky. I was able to come and live with my grandfather, I have a job, and my grandfather looks after Victoria while I'm working. Lots of women aren't as fortunate as I am. They don't have any money. They can't get a job. They don't have a family to go home to. And if you're all alone like that with a little baby, sometimes the only thing you can do is give it up. Try not to blame your mother—she probably did the best she could.'

'She didn't love me! She couldn't have.'

Ashley hesitated, something in her refusing to give the comforting insincere replies that came to mind. 'We don't know that, Tim,' she said slowly. 'Maybe she was so beaten down by the circumstances of her life that she wasn't capable of loving anyone, even herself. Maybe she thought the most loving thing she could do for you was to give you up, because that way you'd have a chance... You may never know the answer.' Again she hesitated, searching for exactly the right words. 'But there are other people in the world who will love you, Tim—if you let them. And you can love them back.'

'Like who?' he said brusquely.

She was not put off by his manner, certain that he genuinely wanted an answer. 'I don't know you very well, but I care what happens to you. I'm really glad to be here with you now. I know Michael cares about you. And Mrs Collins was really upset this evening when she found out you'd gone.'

'Oh.' Into her jacket Tim muttered, 'I'm glad you're here, too.'

It was, for Tim, a huge step. Wisely Ashley said nothing further, simply holding the boy close and hoping some of the warmth of her body was seeping into his. When next she glanced downward, his lashes had fallen to his cheek and he was asleep. She had told him she cared about him, and it had been no lie, for she wanted to give him the day-to-day security that Victoria took for granted. But it would have been more truthful to have said she loved him, she thought with a painful twist of her heart.

She sat very still. Inside her boots her feet were cold, and she wiggled her toes to keep the circulation going. A sharp edge of rock was digging into her spine and her legs were cramped. But somehow she was no longer afraid. Michael would find them. He would not abandon the search until all three of them were safe.

CHAPTER EIGHT

ASHLEY was not wearing her watch and could not judge the passage of time. But the minutes crept by, the snow fell, and the wind gusted through the tree-tops. She was half asleep herself when a familiar and longed-for voice overrode the sounds of the storm and drove the mists of sleep from her brain. 'Ashley! Where are you?'

As she jerked upright, Tim muttered fretfully, 'What's wrong?'

'It's Michael.' She raised her voice. 'We're up here!' Reaching for the flashlight, she waved it back and forth.

She heard the scrape of his boots on the rocks, and his grunts of exertion. Then he had hauled himself up on the plateau and for a blinding moment shone his torch full in her face. She closed her eyes, flinching from the brightness, and felt him gather her and Tim into a rough embrace. 'Oh God, I'm glad I found you! When you weren't down in the caves I thought you were lost, Ashley.'

'No, I'm safe,' she said foolishly, giving him a smile of pure happiness and reaching up to touch his face with her gloved hand. 'Are you all right?'

'Sure,' he said; later she was to realise that he had not been strictly truthful. 'And Tim—are you okay?'

Tim appeared to be tongue-tied. Ashley said calmly, 'He has either a sprained or a broken ankle. The right one. That's why we're up here.'

Michael made a quick examination, while Ashley unashamedly let her eyes linger on his face. Snow was caught in his eyebrows and moisture beaded his cheeks; assuming he was intent upon his task, she was taken by surprise when he looked up to catch her staring at him. The brilliance of flame flared in his blue eyes. He kissed her, a brief hard kiss, then sat back on his heels. 'A bad sprain rather than a break, I think. We've got two choices. We can wait here until the police find us—Beth will have phoned them by now—or we can try and make our way back at least as far as the path from the meadow . . . Frankly, I think we should head out. If we stay here, there could be quite a delay. The wind's died down a bit, but it's still pretty cold. And the sooner we get Tim some medical attention, the better.'

'I tried to lift him, but I couldn't,' volunteered Ashley.

'If you can help to hoist him on my back, I'll piggyback him out,' said Michael. 'The worst part will be getting down to the ground. Once we're on the level, there'll be no problem.'

The next few minutes were to remain in excruciating detail in Ashley's memory for a long time. It was impossible to lift Tim on to Michael's back without hurting the boy; a stubborn and very masculine pride kept Tim from screaming again, but twice he whimpered between his teeth, and his face was as white as the snow that whirled around them when he was finally secured on the breadth of Michael's shoulders. Ashley went first, holding the torch to light Michael's way, supporting him and his helpless burden whenever she could. Because she was paying more attention to them than to herself, she slipped twice, banging her elbow and knee the first time, scraping her cheek the second. Once Michael almost fell on top of her; Tim whimpered again, and her soul cringed within her.

Michael slid the last five or six feet, landing with a jarring thud on the ground. She heard his gasp, and said sharply, 'Did you hurt your knee?'

'It's okay,' he grunted. 'Let's go.'

'Maybe I could carry him for a while now that we're down the cliff.'

'Ashley, get moving.'

She compressed her lips in frustration, not at all sure that she could have carried Tim, but terrified that

Michael might do permanent damage to his knee. She helped all she could, holding branches up and keeping the flashlight trained on their path; but it seemed like very little. Although she could see that Michael was limping, favouring his bad leg, she dared not offer her help again.

The journey seemed endless. But eventually, fluttering around the trunk of a birch tree, Ashley saw a tiny strip of red plastic. They had reached the path that led to the meadow. The going was easier now, earth and the softness of fallen needles under their feet rather than jagged rocks; and gradually the angry voice of the river was softened by distance to a pleasant murmur. The path widened. Clumps of grass poked through the snow and the incline steepened. Then, high on the hill, a cluster of lights appeared. Said Ashley redundantly, 'The police.'

Michael made no comment, stubbornly limping up the hill to meet them. Ashley would have preferred to wait. Instead she shone the torch on the grass and traipsed up the slope behind him.

All at once they seemed to be surrounded by people, although afterwards she was to realise there had actually been only three men and a dog. Tim was carefully taken from Michael's shoulders and put in a fireman's lift between two hefty policemen. Then they all trudged up the hill, Ashley dimly aware that Michael was explaining the situation to the third policeman. There was more confusion in the house: the hallway crowded with over-large men, Mrs Collins fussing around, Mr Parker, the young teacher, miraculously producing big mugs of tea. It was decided that Mr Parker would take Tim to the nearby cottage hospital for X-rays; the three policemen and the dog departed; Mrs Collins was despatched to phone Matthew and explain that Ashley would not be driving home in the snow; and Michael said wearily, putting down his half-empty mug, 'Let's go to my place until Tim gets back—tea's all very well, but I could do with a drink. In the meantime I'll get Beth to make you up a bed in the guest room over here.' He grinned crookedly. 'Much as I would like it, you'd better not stay in my wing of the house.'

He looked exhausted, his eyes sunk deeply in their sockets, his face without colour. Ashley knew he was trying hard not to limp; but she had only to look at his drawn features to realise he was in pain. She smiled at him. 'A drink sounds wonderful.'

They went out of the front door into the cold November night again. Filled with an obscure need to touch Michael, Ashley tucked her hand into his sleeve: a simple action, but one which stopped him in his tracks. He said roughly, 'I'm sorry you got involved in this. It's been one hell of an evening for you.'

'I'm not sorry.'

With a bitterness that shocked her, Michael added, 'Three years ago I could have run a mile with that kid on my back. And now look at me—I can hardly stand up!'

There was a wealth of pent-up frustration in his voice. Ashley said sharply, 'Stop feeling sorry for yourself!'

'*Sorry* for myself? You think——'

'For goodness' sake, if we're going to argue, let's go indoors. I've had enough fresh air tonight to last me the rest of the winter.'

For a moment she thought he was going to lash back at her. However, he turned away, heading towards the side door, his shoulders hunched. He unlocked the door and gestured for her to go ahead of him. It was warm inside, and very peaceful. A bowl of mixed flowers at the foot of the stairs reflected the colours of the Persian rug; otherwise it was all as she remembered it.

She said flatly, 'Sit down and let me take your boots off.'

He pulled off his hat, the front of his hair damp and curling. 'I'm quite capable of taking off my own boots.'

'I'm sure you are—but it would be nice if you'd let

me do it for you. I know damn well your knee is half killing you, Michael Gault, so stop pretending that it isn't.'

Glaring at her, he snarled, 'What are you trying to do—rub it in? Do you realise I can't even carry a ten-year-old kid any more?'

'So *what*? Do you think I care?'

'Most women don't want a man who's physically incapacitated.'

'Then maybe I'm not most women.' Scarcely realising what she was revealing about herself, she swept on, 'David was in marvellous physical condition. He no doubt could have leaped up and down that cliff face half a dozen times with Tim on his back. He also was the kind of person who wanted me to destroy the child that we'd created . . . Don't you see what I'm saying, Michael? Far more important to me than any kind of physical ability is your inner strength. Your integrity. Your concern. All the things that make you the way you are.' Unexpectedly her mouth quirked. 'And, after all, you're not quite in your dotage—you did carry Tim three-quarters of the way home, didn't you?'

Michael was looking understandably dazed. 'Ashley——'

Suddenly embarrassed that she had shown so much feeling, she muttered, 'Becky-Cynthia, more likely.'

'No. Ashley.' His own smile lit up his face. 'My beautiful, passionate Ashley who's put me properly in my place.'

'Well, it was your pride that was hurt, wasn't it?' she mumbled. 'You didn't think you were the big macho hero you should have been . . . I don't feel the slightest bit beautiful, and my feet are cold.'

He sat down rather abruptly on the bench by the front door. 'You were going to take my boots off.'

'Oh, yes.' She knelt down, bending her head so that he could not see that she was blushing, and busied herself with the laces of his boots. She helped him ease his feet out of them and then quickly took off her own, hanging her wet jacket on the door knob. 'Where's that drink?' she said lightly.

'Come into the living room and I'll light the fire. How about a hot whisky with honey?'

'Sounds wonderful!'

He touched a match to the neatly laid paper and kindling in the big stone fireplace, and drew the curtains. Ashley was standing awkwardly by the fire. No real heat was coming from it yet; her hands were still cold. Giving her a keen look, Michael said gently, 'You scraped your cheek.'

'On the cliff. When we were getting Tim down.'

'And you look half frozen.'

She dropped her eyes. 'I'll be all right.'

He took one of her hands in his, rubbing her ice-cold fingers, and briefly rested his palm against her cheek. 'You *are* half frozen! And if your jeans are as damp as mine, they feel bloody awful. Ashley, why don't you have a hot bath? You can borrow something of mine to wear while your clothes dry.'

It sounded like a heavenly idea. She said warily, 'No pass?'

'No pass.'

'Okay.'

The bathroom, which was tiled in deep blue, had a sunken tub, an array of soft yellow and blue towels, and gracefully spreading ferns under the twin skylights. An adjoining door led into Michael's bedroom. Obediently Ashley followed him in there. While he opened the closet door, looking at the contents in faint perplexity, she snatched a quick glance around the room. It too had a fireplace, flanked by bookshelves and comfortable armchairs. The carpet and woodwork were palest ivory, the walls a soft shade of rose. Deep rose-coloured cushions were carelessly flung on the bed.

'Anything of mine is going to be far too big for you,' Michael said.

Hurriedly she looked into the closet, standing no closer to him than was strictly necessary. Business suits, sports clothes, casual wear, all tidily arranged on hangers. She grabbed a green and red plaid woollen bathrobe, a very utilitarian garment, from its hanger. 'This will do,' she decided.

She locked herself in the bathroom, filled the tub with steaming hot water, and climbed in. She soon stopped shivering, and the soreness began to seep from her muscles. Lazily she soaped herself, then let the water gurgle down the drain. The towels were thick and fluffy; she felt a great deal better. With a feeling of peculiar intimacy she dusted herself with some of Michael's Chanel powder before brushing her hair and pulling on the robe. The sleeves came to her fingertips and the hem to mid-calf; she had to remove the belt from its loops or it would have encircled her hips rather than her waist. Not by any stretch of the imagination could it be called a sexy garment, she decided as she grinned at herself in the mirror. She looked like the waif from the storm rather than Playmate of the Year.

Michael, who had changed into navy slacks and a turtleneck sweater, was stretched out on the carpet in front of the fire, and raised his glass to her in casual salute as she entered. Ashley sat down with her knees bent under her, leaning on one palm, and picked up her glass from the hearthstone. The flames had gained hold now, an incandescent, never-still sheet of orange. The wood crackled and spat. Dreamily she gazed into the coals, sipping her drink, totally relaxed.

When Michael spoke, it was almost as if it was part of the dream. 'The firelight's shining in your hair,' he said softly.

She answered, naïvely, 'I can see the flames reflected in your eyes.'

'The flames of passion, my dear,' he said with a lazy grin.

She gave a gurgle of laughter. 'You don't look the slightest bit passionate.'

'One word from you and I shall ravish your body.'

Ashley flushed. 'No passes, you said.'

'So I did. What a pity.' For a moment he gazed into the glowing heart of the fire. Then he brought his eyes back to Ashley. The laughter had gone from them. He said, almost emotionlessly, 'You must know I love you, Ashley. I want to marry you.'

A log shifted on the grate, sending a shower of sparks spiralling up the chimney. Ashley said blankly, 'You *what*?'

He made no move to close the distance between them or to touch her. 'You heard me—I love you. I want to marry you.'

With a flicker of irritation she replied, 'You sound about as excited as if you were giving the latest quotes on the stock market.'

'Don't worry—I have emotion enough for the two of us.' Deliberately he let his eyes travel over the length of her body from her shining fall of hair to her small, bare feet, and for Ashley it was almost as if he had undressed her, so intimate was his gaze. 'And passion enough for two,' he added. 'But I don't want to frighten you, Ashley. Old-fashioned as it sounds, I want you to know that my intentions are strictly honourable . . . there'll be no repeat of David. Not from me. I want to marry you first—and then we'll make love.'

She seized upon the only concrete objection she could think of. 'But what about Victoria?'

'I told you some time ago I was in love with Victoria.' He gave her another of those devastating, lazy smiles.

'Do be serious, Michael!' She took a long gulp of her drink to still her quivering nerves.

He said levelly, 'If you were agreeable, I'd like to adopt Victoria. Give her my name just as I would give it to you. Make her my daughter legally. Because I love her, I don't have to tell you that.'

A father for Victoria. Hastily Ashley corrected herself. *Michael as Victoria's father.* She said in a low voice, knowing it for the truth, 'I would trust you with Victoria. Absolutely and without reserve. I think you'd make her a wonderful father.' She looked straight into the vivid blue depths of his eyes. 'I can't imagine saying that to anyone else that I know or have ever known.'

'Including David . . .?'

'Including David.'

It was not often that she saw Michael at a loss for words. He was staring at her as if he had never seen her before, and something in his face made her want to cry. He made a small, helpless gesture with his free hand. 'That was a beautiful thing to say.'

'I meant every word of it.' She peered at the carpet, her hair falling to hide her face. 'But I can't get married just to give Victoria a father.'

'Let me add something else. Were we to marry, Ashley, I'd ask you if we could adopt Tim as well.'

Her jaw dropped. As if Tim was in the room with her, she felt again the bird-like fragility of his shoulder under her hand, saw the guarded grey eyes, and heard him say, *Thank you, Ashley . . . I'm glad you're here.* She closed her eyes, knowing in a frightening rush of emotion how much she wanted to give Tim the love and security he had always lacked and so sorely needed. What joy it would be to have him as their son, under their roof, day after day, week after week, year after year. She said faintly, 'That's blackmail.'

'No, it's not. It's just another factor to consider, that's all.'

'You're sounding like a stockbroker again.'

'I'm trying to keep emotion out of this. Sure, I love Tim. And sure, I'd like him to have a proper home. But I don't think it would be very fair of me to ask you to marry me without raising all these other issues.'

She had the sensation that she was being drawn deeper and deeper into a web of words that were ensnaring her against her will. 'Michael, I can't marry you just to provide Victoria with a father and Tim with a mother! That's not why people get married.'

He put his drink on the stone hearth, got to his feet and walked over to her. Bending, he rolled back the cuffs of the robe and took her hands in his, pulling her to her feet. Then he said, 'Why do people get married, Ashley?'

She could feel her heart pumping in her breast; it was not the propitious moment to remember that under the soft woollen folds of Michael's robe she was naked. 'They get married because they love each other,' she said, too loudly. 'But——'

'Exactly.' His eyes were trained on her upturned face. 'I love you. And I'm almost sure you love me. But because of what happened with David, you're scared to admit it. You think if you say, *I love you*, that I'll vanish in a puff of smoke.'

'That's ridiculous!' she said crossly. 'Hasn't it occurred to you that I simply may not love you?'

'When you were yelling at me about my knee an hour or so ago, you didn't sound exactly detached!'

'I was angry with you, that's all.' Vainly she tried to pull her hands free.

'You were certainly angry. But the reason you were angry is because you care about me.'

'All right, so I care about you,' she retorted. 'That's not the same as being madly in love with you.'

'It's a darned good beginning.' He finally released her, but only to slide his hands up the length of her arms to her shoulders. With his thumbs he gently kneaded the soft, rounded flesh. 'Do you remember the evening we said goodnight by the car? I asked you to pretend you were in love with me, remember? Let's do it again. Put your arms around my neck and kiss me if you loved me, Ashley.'

She was too upset to be polite. 'Why? So you can prove that I—I want you?'

'Just so.'

'That's lust, not love.'

'It's not lust when emotions are involved,' Michael said harshly. 'You trust me, you care about me, you desire me—don't you think that adds up to three more words? You love me.'

'What is this, a scientific treatise on the nature of love?' she said nastily, knowing with a sinking feeling that she was fighting a losing battle.

'Put your arms around my neck, Ashley. And kiss me.' Nonplussed, she gazed up at him. He gave her no quarter, the blue eyes relentless, the mouth unsmiling.

Damn you, Michael Gault, she thought furiously. *Damn you, damn you ... because you've got me cornered. Either I climb on the fence to balance between heaven and earth like that little girl so long ago, or I call myself a coward. And you know perfectly well that's the choice I'm faced with. Well, you asked for it!*

He said very softly, 'I said you were to pretend you love me. Right now you look as if you'd like to stick a knife in my ribs.'

'I'll try to do better,' she said with mock meekness, her eyes glittering.

'Becky-Cynthia's back!'

Suddenly she was enjoying herself. 'By no means. Becky-Cynthia doesn't like men, remember? I'm Ashley, Michael.' She pouted at him provocatively, running her finger along the cleanly sculptured line of his mouth. Passion flared in his eyes like the flames of the fire, and between one moment and the next her lighthearted game changed to reality. Her heart was racing in her breast as she raised her mouth to his.

It was a kiss that turned her world upside down, for in it was both domination and surrender, taking and giving. She clung to him helplessly, scarcely able to breathe, dimly aware of his hands running over her body in frantic haste. He must have discovered she was naked under the garment she was wearing, and he must equally have sensed her inability to impede him. His mouth left hers to travel the length of her neck, his fingers pushing the robe aside to expose the delicate arc of her collarbone and the shadow between her breasts. Then he had lowered her to the floor, her hair in pale disarray against the carpet. Baring her breasts, he brought the shining, silvery strands forward to cover them again. 'You don't know how I've longed to do that,' he said huskily.

It was all happening too fast. Uncertainly Ashley whispered his name. 'Michael . . .'

The shadow of her nipple showed through the silken hair. He bent to take it in his mouth, his tongue circling her flesh in slow, sensuous circles. She felt the first touch of wonderment, together with an insistent, aching need for more. But at the same time his body was crushing her, his thighs pinning her to the floor so that she could not move, and even more insistently fear mounted. Just so had David's body thrust her down so many months ago, to bring her only pain and a shameful sense of inadequacy. As Michael's hand moved to cup her other breast, caressing its softness, she said raggedly, 'Michael, please . . .'

He must have misinterpreted her. Fumbling for the belt of the plaid gown, he moved his hips against hers, so that she felt his pulsing need of her. She grabbed his shoulders to push him away, and heard him murmur, 'I love you, Ashley. My beautiful Ashley . . .'

She put all her strength into one convulsive heave of her body. 'Don't!' she cried. 'Please, don't!'

He froze. 'What's the matter? Did I hurt you?'

'No. No—I just want you to stop.' She rolled free of him, sitting up and pulling the neckline of the robe together to conceal her breasts.

'Ashley, I love you——'

She covered her ears with her hands, her eyes anguished. 'Don't say those words—I don't want to hear them!'

Brutally he pulled her hands down. 'You *will* hear them.'

Mind and body in a turmoil of conflicting emotions, she cried, 'You're using those words to get your own way.'

'What the hell do you mean?'

'You want my body, you desire me, so you figure you'll pretty it all up by telling me you love me—that way I'll fall flat on my back and give you everything you want. You don't love me—you only want me in your bed. So why dress it up as anything else?'

Michael's face was very pale. 'That's not true, Ashley. I do love you. And part of loving you is wanting you—a very legitimate part.'

She was beside herself with rage, trembling all over. 'You're all alike, you men—I hate you!'

'I'm not like David—I swear I'm not!'

She scrambled to her feet. 'I don't want your love— do you hear me? Any more than I want your body. I don't *want* them!'

Michael did not get up. Stricken to stillness, he remained crouched on the carpet. His eyes were strangely vacant.

Ashley's words seemed to hover in the air between them. Fighting to control her breathing, her fists clenched at her sides, she heard them echo in her brain. Cruel words. Angry words. But truthful, she thought despairingly. How could she have said otherwise? . . . If only he would move, or say something. His eyes reminded her of those of a young mother at the hospital where Victoria had been born, who had just been told her baby had died: blank with shock, yet with the shattering knowledge of pain hovering behind the shock. She opened her mouth to say something, anything, but the words would not come.

Into the bitter, waiting silence the telephone rang. Automatically Michael's head swung in its direction. Yet it rang twice more before he got to his feet; his limp was more noticeable than usual as he crossed the room to the hall. The ringing stopped. She heard his voice speak briefly, then he came back into the living room. 'Tim's back from the hospital. I'm going to see him. You can get dressed and Beth will show you your room.'

'His ankle—was it broken?' she faltered.

Michael frowned, obviously focusing on her words with difficulty. 'No, only sprained.'

Unconsciously Ashley stretched out an imploring hand. But Michael had pivoted, and did not see it. His footsteps crossed the hall. The front door opened and closed.

Her hand fell to her side. She felt as though she had murdered something alive and vulnerable, as though her words had destroyed, irreparably, something beautiful that had been fashioned with love. All the excuses and rationalisations in the world could not banish the pain she had inflicted on Michael.

Her eyes burning with unshed tears, Ashley left the living room, locating her jeans in the dryer in the utility room. It seemed a horrible invasion of privacy to go back into Michael's bedroom, for she, of all people, had no right there. Her fingers awkward with haste, she got dressed, and carefully replaced the robe on its hanger in the closet. About to turn away, she saw a heap of framed pictures on the floor. The top one was a certificate of some kind, the letters in an elegant calligraphy, the crest painted in glowing colours. She knelt down, her eyes skimming the official phrases. It was Michael's discharge from the police force, an honourable discharge with special commendation for long and difficult service.

Ashley straightened and closed the cupboard door. While she had never taken Wayne's accusations seriously, this was not the right moment to be reminded of Michael's courage and integrity. Switching off the bedroom light, she padded on socked feet back to the hall, pulled on her jacket, boots, and gloves, and left the house.

It was still snowing. She'd better get to the garage early tomorrow, she thought dully, because half of Lower Hampton would be arriving to get their snow tires put on.... The garage seeemed a long way away, and her interest in snow tires was nil.

She ran up the front steps. As she reached for the door knob, the door opened from the inside and Michael stepped out. When he saw her, he checked, then recovered. 'Beth is in the kitchen,' he said in a clipped voice.

'I'm sorry I lost my temper,' said Ashley in a rush.

'You had every right to. I told you I wouldn't make a pass at you, then I fell on you like an animal. Don't worry, it won't happen again.'

There was a cold finality to his tone that terrified her. 'What do you mean?' she stammered.

'I think it would be best if we don't see each other for a while. The last thing I want to do is hurt you or frighten you—yet that's precisely what I did this evening, isn't it? Here, you'd better go in—Beth has a horror of what she calls night air.'

Ashley used the only weapon she could think of. 'Won't I see Tim again either?'

Michael shrugged indifferently. 'If he wants to go to the garage, I'll get Bob Parker to take him.' His face closed against her. 'Goodbye, Ashley.'

Goodbye, not good night. Her throat tight, Ashley whispered, 'Goodbye,' and stepped into the house, carefully closing the door against the ubiquitous night air. It was just as well she had, for Beth Collins was bustling into the hall, smiling brightly.

'Your bed's all ready, dear. And you must be ready for it. Tim's already asleep, poor lamb, but he asked me to say good night to you.'

It was the final straw, that tough, introverted Tim should have thought enough of her to send her a special message. Ashley quavered, 'I think I will go straight to bed—I'm really tired. And I'll have to be up early in the morning to get to work on time. Can you show me the way?'

'Right down this hall, dear, second door on the left. The room has its own bathroom. Sure you don't want anything to eat or drink?'

The thought of either one nauseated Ashley. 'No, thanks. I'll be fine.'

'Good night, then, dear. Sleep well.'

The guest room had pretty floral wallpaper,

cherrywood furniture, and pale blue wall-to-wall carpeting, all of which was wasted on Ashley. She threw her jacket and jeans on an antique chair, set the alarm clock on the bedside table, and climbed into bed. Sleep washed over her in a remorseless black tide, drowning her in its depths.

CHAPTER NINE

THE alarm ripped through a confused dream in which Ashley and her brother Bob were crouched against a cliff face drinking hot whisky while Bob dared her to jump. Her heart pounding, Ashley snapped off the buzzer and sat up. It was still dark, and for a moment she had no idea where she was. Not on the cliff face, that much was sure.

Her eyes grew accustomed to the darkness, and she remembered exactly where she was and why, not a memory she relished. Getting out of bed, she pulled back the curtains. It was no longer snowing. A few stars twinkled in the sky. To the east the horizon had paled to a luminous grey. Time she was on her way.

Moving very quietly, Ashley remade the bed and dressed. Then she tiptoed to the front door, laced up her boots, and left the house, walking as gingerly as she could across the gravelled driveway. The south wing was in darkness. *That's what you wanted, isn't it?*

She scraped the snow from her windshield and rear window, started the Honda, and drove away immediately. It was not particularly good for the engine to do that on a cold morning, but it was infinitely better than running the risk of seeing Michael again.

Only two or three inches of snow had accumulated; while there were icy patches on the main road, it was mostly bare. Ashley drove steadily, keeping her mind on the road, and reached home at the time she would have normally have been getting out of bed. In the kitchen Matthew was stirring the porridge, while Victoria waved her rattle in her chubby fist and gave her mother a wide smile that for the last couple of days had included two tiny, pearl-like teeth.

'Morning, Grandad. Hi, Victoria! Did you sleep

150

well, love? Is the tea made, Grandad? Wonderful, I could do with a cup.'

'You had quite the evening's entertainment,' commented Matthew.

'Indeed we did. I wouldn't want to do that too often, it was horribly cold.' She chatted on about the rescue operation, managing to weave Michael's name into the narrative quite naturally, and starting to feed herself and Victoria at the same time. Matthew put in a few questions, grunted a lot, and said finally, 'With all that going on, guess I don't get my twenty dollars, eh?'

Ashley choked on a mouthful of porridge and turned an interesting shade of red. 'I—I'd forgotten about our bet.'

'So he did ask you,' said Matthew with a self-congratulatory nod. 'Figured he would.'

She would have to be honest, for she'd get no peace until Matthew's curiosity was satisfied. Ashley said hardly, 'Grandad, I'm going to tell you this once, and I don't want you to keep on about it. Michael did ask me to marry him and I turned him down. I'm not in love with him, and I can't marry him just to give Victoria a father.' She seemed to have said that before, she thought wildly. She should get a record made.

Matthew banged his mug on the table, Victoria followed suit with her rattle, and Ashley braced herself. 'You *what*?' he bellowed.

'You heard me,' she answered with commendable patience. 'And no, you're not getting any more details—they're personal.'

Matthew tugged at his moustache. 'I'll phone him up.'

'Don't you *dare*!'

'What's wrong with him?'

'Nothing. He's a fine man,' she said shortly. 'I don't love him, that's all.'

'You'd turn down the Archangel Gabriel! It's time you smartened up, my girl.'

She said fliply, 'It's time I went to work.' She got up,

ruffling Matthew's wiry hair, knowing all too well that his ranting and roaring sprang from a very real affection for her. 'I'll come over for a coffee at ten.'

When she did so, promptly at ten, Matthew's opening words were, 'When are you seeing him again?'

'I presume you mean Michael, do you?' Ashley answered coldly, stirring sugar in her coffee.

'You don't have so many boy-friends that I have to specify them by name.'

'I'm not seeing him at all for a while.'

'Whose idea was that?'

If only her parents hadn't brought her up with such a strict regard for the truth . . . 'His.'

'So it looks as though I won't be seeing him either,' Matthew said in an aggrieved voice. 'I had a couple of tricks up my sleeve for our next chess game.'

The coffee was far too hot. Her face pinched, her voice not quite steady, Ashley said, 'Grandad, may we please drop the subject of Michael Gault?'

'At least you're not indifferent to him—that's something.'

Of all the emotions with which she was struggling, indifference was not paramount. 'I've got ten cars lined up to have their snow tyres installed,' she said weakly. 'That probably happens every year after the first snowfall, does it?'

It snowed again the next day. Matthew contented himself with directing brooding looks in her direction and letting fall a number of interesting facts about star-crossed lovers. Victoria produced her third tooth. Ashley replaced an emergency brake cable, installed a new fan, and did three safety inspections. Michael did not phone.

This became the pattern of her days; her world had narrowed to her work and her family. Before she had met Michael she had been content to have it so. Now there seemed to be a void, a lack of companionship where previously she had been self-sufficient. She missed Michael, missed him cruelly. His unforced affection for Victoria; his man-to-man bonding with Matthew; his laughter, his balanced sense of judgment, his wit ... she missed them all. She wanted to watch him hold Victoria in his arms as naturally as if the child had always belonged there. She wanted to see him walking across the grass with that slight hesitation in his step and his blue eyes smiling at her. Worst of all, she wanted to feel his arms go around her and see the softness in his face before he kissed her ...

She did not understand herself. If it were not for her own actions, Michael would be here, she knew it. It was she who had banished him. So why was she complaining because he had taken her words to heart? She should be pleased that he wasn't bothering her, that he was no longer badgering and importuning her with a love she did not want.

But she was not pleased. She was, she admitted to herself if not to Matthew, miserably unhappy. It did not occur to her that there was no need to admit her misery to her grandfather: that her shadowed eyes, restless movements, and all-too-rare smiles were self-explanatory. She was simply grateful that he appeared to have accepted the status quo, settling back into his routine of whist and poker games and visits to the bookmobile as if Michael had never existed.

About ten days after her last visit to Valleyview Bob Parker phoned her at the garage. 'Ashley? I have to spend the day in Halifax. I'm wondering if I can drop Tim off on the way and pick him up on my way back—about five, say. Would that be convenient? He'd really like to see you.'

It should be Michael phoning ... *oh God*. In a carefully controlled voice Ashley said, 'That would be fine.'

'You sure?'

She dredged up a little more feeling. 'Of course. I'd love to see Tim. Tell him to wear old clothes.'

'That's never a problem with Tim,' chuckled Bob. 'See you later.'

They arrived within the hour. Bob Parker was a pleasant-faced young man whose obvious admiration touched Ashley not at all. Tim followed him into the garage, giving Ashley an awkward, sideways smile, then saying gruffly, 'What are you doing?'

She gave him a quick hug, felt tears burn her eyes, and bent over the motor of a Pontiac Acadian. 'New battery. I'll get you to help me lift out the old one.'

It was mixed blessing spending the day with Tim. Every now and then, as if by habit, his old truculence would surface; but on the whole he was far more open with her than he had ever been, and it was obvious that their conversation amidst the windswept rocks by the river had changed his attitude. He made little jokes, he held Victoria in his lap at lunchtime, letting her tug his bright red hair, he patted Toby and sided with Matthew in a discussion about radial tyres. It was heartwarming for Ashley to see the difference in him; it was also heartrending, for Michael's proposal that they adopt Tim was never far from her mind. It wouldn't happen now; she had seen to that.

When they were back in the garage that afternoon, her elaborately casual question about Michael's well-being brought only an offhand, 'Oh, he's fine. I think the radiator needs topping up.'

It did. She went to get the coolant and tried to think about anything but Michael. It was horrible saying goodbye to Tim at the end of the afternoon, knowing he was going back to Valleyview and she was not. She cried herself to sleep that night and the next morning had to put up with Matthew's growled, 'Don't you think this has gone on long enough? You're wasting away to nothing, girl. Pick up the phone and tell him you want to see him.'

'*He* doesn't want to see me, Grandad. Pass the sugar, please.'

Muttering uncomplimentary remarks under his breath about women in general and Ashley in particular, Matthew did as he was asked. After breakfast Ashley went to work, hoping that nobody would look at her the wrong way, because if they did she would burst into tears. At nine-thirty, when she was in the office totalling up a bill, a car drew up by the gas pumps. Tommy ran outside to look after it. The driver, his back to her, got out of the car. He was tall and broad-shouldered, wearing a red-checked lumberman's jacket; his hair was brown.

Ashley grabbed the edge of the counter, wondering if she was going to faint. It was Michael . . . he had come! The grey November day was suddenly suffused with light, and happiness glowed in her face. What did it matter that she was looking far from her best? Nothing mattered except that Michael was here.

The man turned to face her. He was younger than Michael and even at that distance she could see that his eyes were brown.

The bill was forgotten on the counter. She ran into the garage, locked herself in the tiny washroom, and wept as if her heart would break.

Unfortunately, she decided some time later as she regarded her tear-streaked face in the cracked mirror, hearts did not break. That would be too simple. Life went on as if nothing had happened, and in fifteen minutes she had a valve job to do. *Why don't you quit fooling yourself, Ashley?* she said to herself. *You're in love with Michael. You must be. Why else are you crying your eyes out because you've seen someone who looks like him?*

In retrospect the man had not even resembled Michael that closely; it had been her own overly-vivid imagination that had supplied the likeness. That, and her unacknowledged, desperate need to see him. *I love him,* she thought wonderingly. *I love Michael. All along I've been pretending that I don't. But I do.* For the moment that was enough.

However, as the day wore on, her flood of emotion subsided and her brain started to function again. Why, if she loved Michael, had she adamantly insisted both to him and to herself that she did not? Why had she repulsed him so thoroughly that night by the fire?

Because I was afraid. I was remembering what had happened with David.

But there had been no need to be afraid. She knew that now and should have known it then, for she could not imagine two men more different than Michael and David. Michael would never let her down as David had, it would be totally out of character. To Michael love meant commitment, and commitment meant marriage. No ifs, ands or buts. A perfectly straightforward equation—yet one that she had been too overwrought to understand or to accept.

Her brow wrinkled. Love, commitment, and marriage meant something else, of course: sex. Michael would see sex as a natural and beautiful expression of his love for her, inseparable from the emotion he felt towards her. In theory she felt the same way. In practice she had thrust him away like an outraged virgin. Which she was not.

She remembered the sight of his head against her breast, his hands tangled in her hair, the firelight dancing over them both. She remembered their kiss, and her body trembled. Making love to Michael might be very different from what it had been with David; perhaps the splendour and intimacy of that kiss was the prediction of a greater splendour and a deeper intimacy, beyond her wildest imaginings. Perhaps ... but how could she know? And what if she were wrong? What if she were frigid, as David had so callously suggested? How could she share a bed with Michael if she were unable to respond to him?

She did not know how to answer these questions. She forced her attention back to the work she was doing, and was very quiet that evening. Yet when she woke in the morning, she knew exactly what her course of action was to be. Frightened and happy at the same time, she went to the garage as usual, busied Tommy with rearranging the outdoor display of motor oils and windshield washers, and went to the telephone, dialling Michael's private number.

She had hoped to reach him before he went over to the main house. However, although she let the phone ring five times he did not reply. Picking up the directory, she looked up the number for Valleyview Farm and dialled again. On the second ring Beth Collin's voice said cheerfully, 'Valleyview. May I help you?'

'It's Ashley MacCulloch, Mrs Collins. May I speak to Michael, please?'

'Now, I believe he's somewhere around. Give me a minute to find him, dear. Oh, here he is, with Mr Parker . . . It's Ashley, Mr Gault. She'd like to speak to you.'

Not exactly the privacy Ashley had hoped for. She waited, her mouth dry, and heard Michael say crisply, 'Hello.'

'Michael, it's me—Ashley.' *Your grammar's gone as well as your nerve,* she thought frantically. She plunged on, 'I'm wondering if I could come and see you . . . maybe this evening?'

She could hear boys' voices in the background, then admonishments for silence from Mrs Collins. 'Why?' Michael asked tersely.

'I'd rather not discuss my reasons on the phone. But I really would like to see you—I need to talk to you. If tonight's not convenient, I could make it tomorrow. Or another night.' Her palm was slippery on the receiver, her fingers white with strain.

'No, this evening would be fine. What time?'

'Around eight?' Victoria would be in bed and Matthew's card-playing friends would have arrived by then.

'Fine. Come to my wing of the house.'

'All right. Thank you, Michael.'

'See you, then. Goodbye.'

Slowly Ashley put down the receiver, her heart sinking. There had been no emotion in his voice at all;

he had been as brisk and matter-of-fact as if they had been discussing a business deal. Certainly he had not sounded the slightest bit like a man in love. But she had to go through with it now ... she had committed herself.

When she had woken up this morning, her plan had seemed logical and obvious in the extreme, the only way to remove the barrier between herself and Michael. Now she was not so sure. Maybe her courage would fail by evening, and she would be unable to go through with it. She should have arranged to go right now. Get it over with—like a visit to the dentist, she thought wryly.

On a morning when she would have preferred to be kept busy, there was a dearth of customers. She cleaned out her tool chest, disposed of several days' accumulation of garbage, and unpacked the latest delivery of headlamps and windshield-wipers. By ten o'clock she had run out of things to do. Perched on a stool at the counter, she wrote her dutiful bi-monthly letter to her parents, describing Victoria's new teeth and including a carefully edited account of the escapade with Tim. These letters were never easy to write, although they did, at a superficial level, keep the avenue of communication open, something which seemed important to Ashley.

Sliding off the stool, she decided to walk to the post office. The fresh air would do her good, and anything was better than sitting around worrying herself sick about what might—or might not—happen tonight. Stripping off her overalls, she hung them on a hook by the door, and pulled on her jacket.

The air was more than fresh, it was freezing cold. Ashley hadn't turned her radio on that morning, so she'd missed the weather reports, although she soon decided as she strode along with her hands in her pockets and her shoulders hunched that she didn't need a meteorologist to tell her it was several degrees below zero. Blissfully ignorant of what else she had missed by not listening to the news, she walked past the Darbys' neat little frame house and the untidy tangled woods. Among the trees a flock of crows argued and complained—as vociferously as the ladies of the gardening club, Ashley thought whimsically, knowing how such a comparison would annoy Emma Darby.

The post office was considerably busier than the garage. Ashley nodded and smiled at customers and neighbours, mailed her letter, and took her own mail out of the box, wrinkling her nose at the month-end collection of bills. On the way home she stopped at the general store, intending to pick up only one or two items, ending up, as so often happened, with two bags full of groceries.

She trudged homeward, her cheeks bright pink from the cold, her arms soon aching with strain. If she had wanted distraction from thoughts of Michael, she had got it, she decided, putting the bags on the ground for a minute to flex her shoulders. A car drew up alongside her, a sleek, expensive navy-blue car. The driver leaned over and opened the door on her side. 'Let me give you a lift the rest of the way, Ashley,' Wayne McEvoy said bluffly. 'Those bags look heavy.'

She should have picked up the bags, put her nose in the air and ignored him. Instead the part of her that her mother had never understood could only be amused at his effrontery. And she was perfectly safe now, because he no longer wanted the garage. The phone calls had ceased some time ago and of Willie Budgeon there had been no sign.

She picked up the bags and put them on the back seat. 'I'd appreciate a drive,' she said. 'Just to show there are no hard feelings.'

'Good, good,' Wayne said heartily, waiting until she had shut her door before putting the Lincoln in gear again. 'After all, we can't win 'em all, can we?'

He was wearing another of those hideously expensive overcoats, this one in black and white houndstooth. His scarf was silk, his cap of a type much favoured by the British aristocracy. He did not, she decided critically, have the profile for it. Yet he looked pleased with himself.

'Were you able to buy another garage?' she asked politely.

'None of the other locations were quite what I wanted.'

'I see . . . Would you pass on a message for me?'

'By all means,' he said expansively.

'Tell your friend who made all the phone calls that he really should enlarge his vocabulary. Obscenity does not necessarily have to be boring.'

Wayne's eyes never left the road. 'My dear young lady, what *are* you talking about?'

She dropped all pretence at politeness. 'You know perfectly well what I'm talking about, Wayne. It's just lucky for Grandad and me that proposal for a national park was dropped, isn't it?'

He gave her a distinctly unpleasant smile, glanced at his watch, and flipped on the radio. 'You should listen to the news and keep up to date with what's going on in the world,' he said.

They were approaching the garage, but instead of braking, Wayne was accelerating. Ashley felt a knot gather in the pit of her stomach. 'You can let me off here,' she said.

'Oh, I think we'll go for a little drive instead. Just so you can listen to the news. It's starting now.'

Berating herself for being such an idiot, Ashley saw the garage flash by. There were no cars at the pumps and no sign of Tommy. Smoke climbed lazily from the chimney of her grandfather's house. 'Wayne, let me out!' she snapped. 'And we'll forget this ever happened.'

His answer was to turn up the volume control. More fighting in the Middle East, more bombs in Northern Ireland, more famine in Africa. Then the local news. Rumours of graft in the provincial legislature, a freight train derailed in New Brunswick, and then the statement that Ashley was by now expecting to hear. '. . . Federal officials have announced the site of a new

National Park in Nova Scotia, due to open officially late next summer. The park will encompass over four hundred square kilometres of woodland, including a chain of lakes well-known to canoeists and sports fishermen. Located in the Trout Lake area in the county of——'

Wayne snapped off the radio and said as smoothly as if there had been no break in the conversation, 'So you see, Ashley, I do want the garage, after all. If I can get a monopoly on the gas outlets in the area, I'll make enough money in three or four months in the summer to be able to go south every winter.' He gave that jovial, unconvincing laugh again. 'My wife's always wanted a villa in the Bahamas.'

'Grandad doesn't want to sell,' Ashley said obstinately.

'Oh, I'm sure he'll come around when he realises you're missing. He'll be getting a phone call very shortly.'

The Lincoln was speeding along the highway, the trees and telephone posts flashing past monotonously. 'You'll never get away with it! You've made no attempt at secrecy. All we'll have to do is tell the police about you—kidnapping and extortion are serious crimes.'

'Glad you brought that up, Ashley. You see, I've left a set of instructions with someone whom, obviously, I won't name.' Skilfully he avoided a pothole in the road. 'Should the police become involved, or should my name in any way become associated with our little escapade today, then your daughter, or your grandfather, depending on the circumstances, will suffer an unfortunate accident.' There was real venom in Wayne's voice. 'I can guarantee that. So I advise you, as I shall be advising your grandfather, not to contact the police. You should pay more attention, you know— I thought I'd made all this clear to you once before.'

Ashley stared straight ahead of her, watching the yellow lines in the centre of the road flip by, her hands clenched in her lap. At the thought of anyone laying a

finger on Victoria, she felt such an upwelling of terror
and rage that she was literally speechless.

'I see you get the message,' said Wayne with a
satisfied nod. 'Now where are we? Ah, here's the turn-
off.'

There was no other traffic in sight. He braked sharply
and turned to the left along a straight gravel-surfaced
road unmarked by any signposts. Even the superb
suspension of the Lincoln could not cope with the
combination of frozen ruts and potholes that pitted the
surface of the road; the car lurched along, Ashley
clutching her seat and vainly looking for any signs of
habitation.

There were none. They could have been alone in the
world. The woods had been heavily logged at some time
in the past, brush and rotting stumps scattered over the
ground. The thin trunks of saplings and the white
skeletons of diseased birches stood like the dazed
survivors of a disaster. The sky was a patchwork of
sullen grey clouds.

Ashley had already realised that Wayne did not want
to drive too slowly, or she might risk jumping out of the
car; so he was travelling the rough, pockmarked road
much too fast. As the front wheel rebounded from an
apparently bottomless hole, she said noncommitally,
'You'll break a spring if you keep that up.'

'Then I'll have to get you to fix it, won't I?' he
retorted. He was sweating lightly, she saw with a certain
satisfaction. She knew that his car represented far more
to him than just a means of transportation; it was a
status symbol, a blatant projection of his self-
importance and his newly acquired wealth. He must
hate mistreating it as he now was.

Good, she thought vindictively. *I hope he wrecks it!*

They had travelled four or five miles across the
dismal, mutilated landscape when Ashley spotted a curl
of blue smoke rising from a woodsman's shack set back
from the road. It should have been comforting to see
signs of human habitation in such a bleak place; instead

she felt dread ripple along her nerves. She had known
Wayne had a purpose in mind in travelling this deserted
road, sensing all along that he must have an
accomplice; she had never in her wildest moments
pictured him holding her at gunpoint or tying her to a
tree. Her worst fears were realised as they drew nearer
the shack, a mean, dispirited-looking building con-
structed for utility rather than beauty. A mud-splashed
red truck was parked by the edge of the road, and as
Wayne laid his hand on the horn, Willie Budgeon
stepped outside.

Ashley did not stop to think. Wrenching open the car
door, she flung herself to the ground, curling her arms
and legs towards her chest in an effort to protect
herself. Dimly she heard Wayne yell something. Then
the breath was knocked from her body by the iron-hard
ground, every bone jarred in its socket.

She fought for air, scrambled to her feet, and saw
that Wayne had stopped the car and was running
towards her, his black and white checked arms waving
wildly in the air, his eyes almost popping out of his
head. Swallowing a hysterical giggle, she wheeled and
began to run.

CHAPTER TEN

FEAR giving wings to her feet, Ashley ran back the way they had come. Miraculously she kept her balance as she leaped over ice-covered puddles and criss-crossed tyre tracks. She felt horribly exposed on the road, but the trees were so sparse on either side of it and the undergrowth so thickly tangled that her progress would have been immeasurably slower and she would have been every bit as visible had she taken to the woods.

Behind her she heard shouting and the slam of a car door. Risking a backward glance she saw Wayne driving towards the shack and Willie climbing into the truck. *Willie's coming after you . . . what else did you expect? Wayne might get his coat dirty . . .*

She ran faster, straining every muscle, her blood pounding in her veins. She'd have to leave the road, or Willie would pick her off as easily as a farmer could catch a fear-crazed hen. So she jumped the ditch, a feat she would not have contemplated in cold blood, hauled herself up the far side and began crashing through the bone-dry, thigh-deep brushwood.

Her progress was slow. It was horribly dangerous, for the ground was littered haphazardly with stumps and branches, and a false step would snap her ankle as easily as the dry, brittle wood was snapping beneath her feet. Her boots felt as heavy as lead, while her tortured lungs were gasping for air. Again she snatched a quick look over her shoulder.

Willie had driven the truck along the road and had parked at the place where she had jumped the ditch. He had crossed it himself and was charging through the brush like a bulldozer. Ashley whimpered with fear, frantically searching the landscape for anything that could aid her escape. There was nothing. Nowhere to hide, no other people, nothing but scrawny trees and hacked-off branches. She could hear Willie crashing along behind her and knew he was gaining on her. Putting the last of her energy into a final, desperate spurt of speed, she reached a tiny clump of bare-limbed tamaracks and turned at bay, her chin high, her grey eyes defiant—a pose her brother Bob would have recognised. Be damned if she was going to let Willie catch her from behind, she thought furiously, as if she was a terrified calf to be lassoed and flung to the ground. Be damned if she'd show him she was afraid, either.

He had clearly not expected her action. He stumbled to a halt, his chest heaving, his face unhealthily red. Trying to control the rasping of her own breath, she said caustically, 'You've been smoking too much, Willie. Lead the way—I'll go back with you.' She spoke as if she was conferring a favour on him.

'You little bitch—making me run after you like that!'

'What did you expect me to do?' she flared. 'Walk up to you and shake hands? How do you do and how nice to see you? To hell with that!'

There was a unwilling gleam of admiration in his eye. 'You need a man to tame you, Ashley MacCulloch. And Wayne McEvoy isn't the one to do it.'

'Neither are you. Talking of Wayne, he looks as though he's going to have a fit—we'd better go back.' With a fine assumption of casualness she walked past Willie and began trekking back to the road, where Wayne was standing flailing his arms over his head and shouting something indecipherable—which was probably just as well, Ashley thought. This time she did not have to look back over her shoulder, for she was aware through every nerve in her body of Willie following close behind her. Although she was still their captive, she knew that, psychologically, she had won this round. Now she had to worry about the next one. It might not be as easy.

It was hard to maintain her dignity as she slid down

one bank of the ditch and clambered up the other, finding time to wonder how she had ever managed to jump across it. Standing up, she scowled at Wayne. 'I hope you're having fun,' she said.

He called her an unprintable name. 'Take her back to the shack,' he ordered Willie. 'I'll go and phone. Once the old man's signed the necessary papers, I'll be back. It won't take long—he won't risk anything happening to her.'

Wayne was probably right. Totally frustrated, Ashley was conscious of a strong urge to lie on the ground, drum her heels and scream her head off. There was pitifully little else she could do.

Willie grabbed her sleeve and pulled her towards the truck. 'Get in—and no more funny business!'

As if she had the energy . . . Obediently she climbed in the cab, feeling her legs trembling under her and hoping neither man would notice. Willie got in the driver's seat, inserted the ignition key and started the truck. Bumping and bouncing over the potholes, the truck proceeded back to the little cabin.

There were two small windows set in the front of the cabin on either side of the door, giving it a cross-eyed look. The walls were rough slats, the roof covered with tarpaper. The chimney, which leaned drunkenly to the north, was a rusted piece of metal pipe. But at least it would be warm inside the shack, Ashley thought, trying to be optimistic. Now that she had stopped running, she was shivering. Having decided that it would be sensible not to anger Willie unnecessarily again, she meekly followed him along the mud path to the wooden door, which was hung on three worn hinges with a loop of yellow nylon rope as a handle. The door creaked open, and she stepped inside.

She was greeted by a blast of heat from the cast-iron pot bellied stove at the far end of the single room. A thin stream of steam issued from a battered kettle set in its lid. There was a bunk against the near wall equipped with a mildewed pillow and a none-too-clean quilt. A plank table and a couple of benches completed the furnishings. Ashley was not reassured to see a bottle of whisky set on top of the table, along with a container of water and a metal lunch pail. Without waiting to be asked, she sat down on the bench and held her hands out to the fire.

Willie seemed at a loss to know how to deal with the situation. He made quite a business of shoving a couple of logs from the woodpile in the corner into the lid of the stove. Then he said sourly, 'Want a drink?'

Her mother would have blanched with horror at Ashley's studiedly casual, 'Thanks, Willie.' But Ashley had been thinking. She was sure Wayne would not delay his return to the shack; all she had to do was keep Willie in a pleasant mood—and at a distance—until Wayne came back.

Willie produced two plastic mugs from the lunch pail and poured generous doses of whisky into each, adding equal measures of water. He pushed Ashley's over to her and plunked himself on the other bench, tossing back half the drink in one gulp. Ashley added more water to her own and took a healthy mouthful. Despite her Scottish ancestry, Scotch whisky was far from her favourite form of alcohol. She had always considered that it tasted rather like turpentine and smelled worse. Now, however, she was glad enough of it; if it gave her Dutch courage, that was better than no courage at all. She said calmly, peering into the lunch pail, 'Can I have something to eat? Trying to outrun a truck gives one an appetite.'

'Help yourself.'

There were massive turkey sandwiches wrapped in wax paper, several oranges, and a couple of thick slabs of chocolate cake. 'Who made the cake?' she asked with genuine curiosity. Somehow she could not picture Willie beating eggs and flour together.

'The cook at the lumber camp.'

She bit into a sandwich with gusto. 'They sure feed you well, if this is any example.'

'It's a smart boss who takes the trouble to find a good cook. Keeps the guys happier than any amount of rum.'

It was the longest sentence she had ever elicited from Willie; inadvertently she was reminded of Tim. 'Have you always worked in the woods, Willie?' she asked.

He poured himself another drink. 'Since I was fourteen.'

She set herself to draw him out, knowing in her heart she would be devastated to see Tim at fourteen exposed to the rough-and-tumble of a lumber camp. No doubt Willie at fourteen had been tougher than Tim; but fourteen was still fourteen. She listened sympathetically, eating her way steadily through a second sandwich and a piece of cake which tasted better than any cake she had ever made. From Willie's terse and ungrammatical sentences she got a picture of a father who had used his belt indiscriminately on wife and children, and of a mother who had been glad enough to have one less mouth to feed and one less child underfoot.

Ashley began peeling an orange, digging her nails into the pungently scented skin and passing Willie a couple of sections. 'My parents were just the opposite,' she commented. 'Watching every move I made and hedging me in with rules and restrictions.' She went on to talk about her brothers and her early interest in mechanics. 'My mother would have liked me to sit primly in the parlour and do needlework,' she said, a touch hyperbolically. 'Instead of which I was always getting grease on my clothes and leaving dirty spark plugs in the pockets of my jeans.' She passed Willie two more pieces of the orange, noticing with trepidation that he was well into his fourth drink. *Lumbermen can hold their liquor, Ashley, don't panic.* But Willie had the reputation for turning mean in his cups, and unconsciously her ears were straining for the sound of Wayne's car. Surely he wouldn't be much longer.

Willie got up to put more wood in the fire. Neither his speech nor his movements seemed at all affected by the amount of alcohol he had consumed. But as he came back to the table, he poured another slug of whisky into her mug. 'You're not drinking,' he said roughly.

Trying to look as though she was enjoying it, Ashley took a gulp of whisky, gasping as it bit into her throat and burned its way down to her stomach. Her eyes watering, she spluttered, 'Put some more water in it, Willie—I can't drink it that strong.'

He did not seem to hear her. He was standing very close to her, staring down at her. With a calloused hand he reached out and touched the smooth sheen of her hair, and said thickly, 'Your hair's like the surface of a lake at dawn, all pale gold.'

She gaped up at him, absurdly wanting to put her head in her hands and cry her eyes out. That Willie could produce such a poetic image from the squalor and violence that had ruled so much of his life touched her immeasurably. She said quietly, 'Thank you, Willie—that was a beautiful thing to say.'

All might have been well had Willie sat down again. But in the stove the logs shifted, the wood crackling and spitting out sparks. His eyes flickered in that direction. When they came back to her there was a new purpose in them.

Ashley said levelly, forcing herself not to shrink away from him, 'Do you mind putting a bit more water in my drink?'

She could almost see the alcohol working in his brain. He repeated roughly, 'Beautiful hair . . .'

He was between her and the door. She braced her feet against the floor and said, putting as much authority in her voice as she could, 'Sit down and have another drink, Willie.'

He ignored her, grabbing for her shoulder. She ducked, sliding down the bench and putting the width of the table between them. Then she made one last attempt to appeal to his reason. 'Don't ruin everything,' she pleaded. 'A minute ago I really liked you—don't spoil that.'

'I won't spoil it—it'll be better.'

'No, it won't.'

'C'mon, Ashley—a little kiss won't do any harm.'

But he would not stop there, she knew. Her eyes darkened with the panic of a cornered animal. As he made another lunge for her, she flung the open lunch pail full at him, and it struck his cheek. The remaining sandwich fell from its wrappings, spreading bits of turkey and lettuce all down his shirt. The oranges tumbled to the floor, rolling on the uneven planks.

Naked fury flared in Willie's pale eyes. 'You shouldn't have done that!' His fingers curled around the neck of the whisky bottle, a weapon far more deadly than any lunch pail. 'Get over here, Ashley.'

Behind her the fire seethed and spat in the potbellied stove. She whirled, grabbed the battered metal kettle from the stove and said with a courage born of desperation, 'Stay where you are—or I'll throw this in your face!'

On this deathless line, footsteps thudded up the earthen pathway and the shack door shrieked on its hinges. Like puppets abandoned by their puppeteers, Willie and Ashley stood frozen, Willie still clutching the half-empty bottle of whisky, Ashley brandishing the steaming kettle. Into the sudden dead silence Michael entered. His fists were clenched, his eyes rinsed to a clear, dangerous blue: a figure, had Ashley but known it, whom certain shady characters across the country would have recognised and avoided at all costs.

Then, simultaneously, three things happened. Ashley put the kettle back on the stove because its handle was burning her palm, Willie dashed the bottle against the edge of the table so that it smashed in a shower of whisky and pieces of glass, and Michael let the door creak shut behind him. 'Stay out of the way, Ashley,' Michael said evenly. He was, she saw incredulously, thoroughly enjoying himself.

The next two or three minutes were noisy, brutal, and destructive. The neck of the whisky bottle, knocked from Willie's grasp by a vicious sideswipe of Michael's palm, shattered the window on its way outdoors, adding to the broken glass on the floor. A chair disintegrated into its component parts when Willie attempted to brain Michael with it and hit the wall instead, for Michael, mysteriously, was not where he should have been. But then Michael tripped over an orange, crashing into the table. Fortunately Willie's fist did not connect with Michael's skull; instead it splintered two of the slats that made up the wall. Willie's swear-word made Ashley's eyes widen with a kind of horrified amusement that her mother would have deplored; wisely she was following Michael's advice and had crouched in the corner by the woodpile, a log in one fist in case she should have to go to Michael's rescue.

The log was not needed. Willie, off balance, presented a perfect target even to Ashley's amateur eyes. Michael's fist connected with a thud worthy of Sylvester Stallone. Willie collapsed in an untidy heap on the floor, his breath escaping from his body in a diminishing hiss.

Ashley should, no doubt, have emulated Willie by collapsing at Michael's feet, although in a flood of grateful female tears rather than unconsciousness. Instead she said crossly, 'You didn't need to hit him *that* hard.'

'Ingrate! Here I am endangering life and limb to rescue you from the villain of the piece, and all you do is complain about how hard I hit him!' His blue eyes were reckless with laughter and with some other emotion Ashley could not analyse.

'He isn't really a villain.' She sighed. 'I almost found myself liking him a little while ago.'

'You didn't look as though you were liking him very much when I arrived. Or do you always wave kettlesful of boiling water in the faces of your friends?'

She said limpidly, 'I put the kettle down when you arrived.'

'So you did. No doubt I should seize my opportunity—in case you change your mind.' Stepping over the recumbent Willie, Michael put his arms around Ashley and kissed her. Possessiveness, desire, the male pride of the victor, were all there in the imprint of his mouth on hers. Her response was direct and primitive; they were lost to everything but each other when the door squealed open again and Matthew stepped over the threshold.

'What's going on here?' he demanded. 'You were supposed to let me know when the coast was clear.'

Michael raised his head long enough to say succinctly, 'I forgot.' Then he kissed Ashley again.

Said Matthew, regarding Willie with interest, 'He's coming to.'

That did get Michael's attention. With scant ceremony he pushed Ashley away. Willie was stirring, muttering something under his breath. His eyelids twitched.

'Pass the rope,' Michael ordered.

From around his waist Matthew looped a length of nylon rope and gave it to Michael, who tied Willie's hands behind his back with brisk efficiency. Matthew also had a hunting knife hanging from his belt loop.

'You forgot the shotgun, Grandad,' Ashley said with pardonable sarcasm.

'It's in the car. Michael wouldn't let me bring it to the shack,' Matthew said in an offended voice.

Her mind made the leap from shotgun to kitchen wall, and with a sickening lurch of her heart she remembered the two players who were absent. All the farcical elements of the past few minutes dropped from her mind. 'Wayne's not here!' she gasped, the colour draining from her cheeks. 'Victoria—you didn't leave Victoria alone, Grandad? Wayne said if we called the police, he'd send someone to—to . . .' She couldn't even put Wayne's threat into words.

'Course I didn't leave her alone.' Matthew gave her a fiendish grin. 'I took her to Emma Darby's.'

'Where?'

'You heard. Thought it would do Emma good— soften her up a bit. I don't reckon the person's born yet who can resist my great-granddaughter.'

'But what about Wayne?'

'It'd take a better man than Wayne McEvoy to get past Emma Darby.'

Helplessly Ashley leaned against the wall and began to laugh, a laugh that had more than a trace of hysteria in it. 'Next thing you know, I'll be asked to join the garden club!'

On the floor Willie groaned, tried to move his hands, and opened a single baleful eye. Michael said crisply, 'Matt, you'd better take Ashley to the car. Wayne should be back any minute.' He eyed Willie with disfavour. 'And in the meantime I have something to say to this fellow.'

'You won't hit him again, will you?' protested Ashley.

'I'm not in the habit of hitting people who are tied up,' Michael responded drily. 'Get moving—I don't want you here when Wayne arrives.'

She gazed at him in perplexity. He was wearing the outfit she had come to know so well, dark cords and sweater and the red-checked lumberman's jacket. His lean body was perfectly relaxed, nor had he once raised his voice. Yet he somehow gave the impression of a toughness and of a totally professional competence that she had to respect. She said slowly, 'You're having a great time.'

'Of course I am. Feel as though I'm back in the trenches again.'

She looked him straight in the eye. 'I'm glad you arrived when you did. Thank you.'

'It had all the elements of classic melodrama, didn't it? Hero to the rescue of the golden-haired heroine . . . who is then supposed to fall into his arms and declare her undying love for him.'

Forgetting their listeners, she said impudently, 'That comes later.'

'Tonight?' said Michael with a dangerous gleam in his eye.

'Oh, that's right—we do have a date, don't we?' As if she could have forgotten.

'You're damn right we do. Matthew's babysitting, I told him so. Now move it, Ashley!'

To her own surprise as much as to his, she obeyed him instantly, taking Matthew's arm and leading him outside. Matthew went with a touch of reluctance, which disappeared as soon as they got outside: from some distance away across the flat landscape they both heard the sound of a car approaching. Swiftly Matthew ducked his head back into the shack, said, 'Wayne's coming,' then grabbed Ashley's sleeve. 'Come on. The car's up the road beyond the bend. Michael wanted it out of sight of the cabin.'

She jogged along behind him, her mind teeming with questions even as her leg muscles protested violently at the exercise. In a couple of minutes she saw the car, cunningly hidden by a straggly clump of spruce trees. They both climbed in, Matthew closing his door with exaggerated quietness and Ashley following suit. The shotgun, she saw, was lying across the back seat. 'Now,' she said grimly, 'I want to know what's been going on. How did you get here so quickly? And why has Wayne come back?'

Matthew settled himself in the seat, drew out his pipe and began tamping in some new tobacco from his chamois pouch. 'Well now . . . apparently you phoned Michael this morning.'

It was not the opening she had expected. 'I did, yes,' she stumbled. 'But what's that got to do with it?'

'Guess you must have roused his curiosity. He arrived at the garage wanting to see you. But you weren't there, and all Tommy knew was that you'd gone to the post office. When you didn't come back we started to worry. Michael checked at the post office and the grocery store. You'd been there, but well over half an hour ago. He was in a real state, I'll tell you. Then the phone rang—it was Wayne. I was to sign documents for the sale of the garage and then you'd be returned, safe and sound.' Matthew lit a match and drew gustily on his pipe. 'You can imagine how I felt about that!'

'I can indeed. So what did you do?'

'I grabbed Victoria's rattle out of her hand, she started to scream, and I told Wayne to hold on to the phone a minute, she'd fallen and hurt herself. Then I told Michael what was going on. He suggested I stall. So I told Wayne I'd meet him at the West Hampton turn-off at lunchtime. He wasn't very pleased, wanted me to meet him right away, but I told him it was the best I could do.'

'Is Victoria back on speaking terms with you?'

'Only just. Stubborn little cuss—like her mother.'

'Like her great-grandfather, you mean. So then what?'

'Then we got lucky. When Michael was driving past this road on his way to the garage, he'd seen Wayne's car going along it. Didn't know it was Wayne's car, of course, but he noticed it because it wasn't the kind of vehicle you'd expect to see on a logging road. He mentioned it to me, I recognised the description, and we were away. Took Victoria up to Emma Darby's and drove up here. Wayne's coming back here to get you—and no doubt to get Willie as well. He's due for a surprise, isn't he?'

She would not want to be Wayne walking unsuspectingly into the shack to find Willie trussed up on the floor and Michael waiting with that dangerous glint in his eyes. 'Serves him right. He was so horrible about Victoria—he really frightened me.'

'Michael'll fix him, don't you worry. He's quite the guy, is Michael. I was glad today he was on my side . . . he'd put the fear of God in me if he wasn't. Mind you, a lot of that was because it was you who was in danger. Can't figure out why you won't marry him, Ashley.'

'Grandad, I——'

'You got burned once, I know. You never say much

about Victoria's father, so I figure he wasn't that good to you. Don't want to judge the rest of the world by him, though. 'Specially not Michael. He'd be good to you, I'd bet my bottom dollar on it.' Emotion roughened Matthew's speech. 'It's a fine life when you're married to the right person. I was for nigh on thirty years. The loneliness half kills you when they're gone, but I wouldn't trade that thirty years for anything on earth.'

'Oh, Grandad . . .' Ashley patted his knee. 'If I did get married, you'd be left on your own again.'

'I managed before, I can manage again. Be worth it to know you were happy.'

She fumbled in the pocket of her jeans for a handkerchief and blew her nose. 'I've been happy with you.' She gave a weak smile. 'We're beginning to sound like a couple of characters in a soap opera, aren't we? We need a violin tremolo in the background.'

Matthew rolled down the car window. 'Hush a minute—sounds like Wayne's leaving.'

It was the slam of a car door that had alerted Matthew. As an engine roared into life, Ashley commented with professional interest, 'He's got a heavy foot on the accelerator. He must be angry.' They sat listening as the sound faded into the distance. Then Michael walked up the road behind them and got in the back seat of the Honda. Ashley twisted to face him. 'You look very pleased with yourself,' she said.

He grinned. 'We can go back now. Time we rescued Victoria from the clutches of Emma Darby.'

'Or the other way around.' She could contain herself no longer. 'What did you *do*? Where's Willie?'

'Wayne is driving Willie back to the camp. No doubt between the two of them they can hatch up a story to explain Willie's black eye.'

'Michael, don't be aggravating—what did you say to them?'

Michael sobered. 'First of all, there's no accomplice who's going to harm Victoria—that was pure fabrication on Wayne's part. Secondly, it's been made very clear to him that he will never be the owner of the garage and that at even the slightest hint of any trouble in the future, a detailed report of today's events will be sent to the police. You won't be hearing any more from Wayne McEvoy, I guarantee it.'

Ashley looked at him, as much impressed by the gaps in the story as she was by what Michael had said. 'Strong arm tactics, eh?' she murmured.

'You could say that,' replied Michael with a noticeable lack of repentance. 'They worked, anyway.'

'What about Willie's truck?'

'They'll have to get it later. Willie was in no shape to drive.'

She had to smother a smile, so self-satisfied did Michael look. 'You should be ashamed of yourself,' she said severely.

'No doubt.' He glanced at his watch. 'I've got to get back to Vallyview. If you reverse, Matthew, you can turn in front of the cabin.'

It was the logical opportunity for Ashley to ask why he had come to the garage in the first place. But she did not dare. Not with Matthew listening to every word, and with the knowledge of her plan for the evening hovering in the back of her mind. She was beginning to wonder if she would have the courage to go through with it; what had seemed like an eminently sensible idea at eight o'clock this morning now seemed utter madness.

CHAPTER ELEVEN

MATTHEW dropped Michael off at the garage, where the jeep was parked in all its battered glory. With a casual, 'Thanks, Matthew. 'Bye, Ashley, see you this evening,' Michael got out of the car and limped over to the jeep.

Matthew did not wait to see him leave. Driving back on to the highway he proceeded to the Darbys' trim little house, where he parked the car and pronounced, 'I brought Victoria here. You go and get her.'

'Thanks a lot!' It was one thing to wave a kettle of boiling water under Willie Budgeon's nose, another to face Emma Darby. Ashley walked up the path, which was neatly bricked in three symmetrical rows, and pushed the highly polished brass doorbell.

Mr Darby opened the door, giving Ashley the best approximation of a real smile she had ever seen on his face. 'Come in. What a dear little girl she is—Emma's just changing her.'

Victoria was lying on her back on the kitchen table, gurgling and cooing cherubically, for all the world as if she was doing a television ad endorsing the disposable diaper Emma was pinning on her. It was plain that Mrs Darby was no more immune to Victoria's charm than was Ashley, for a fatuous smile was spread over Emma's face and she was replying to the juicy gurgles in what was undoubtedly baby talk. When she saw Ashley, she blushed and said very briskly, 'Back already?'

'Thank you very much for looking after her, Mrs Darby. It was very kind of you,' Ashley said awkwardly.

'It was a pleasure. It's been a long time since I've looked after a little baby, I'm glad I haven't lost the touch.' She inclined her head regally. 'In the spring you must bring her to one of our garden club meetings.'

Duly aware of the honour being bestowed upon her, Ashley said faintly, 'Thank you, that would be very nice.' Although if Victoria showed as much enthusiasm for crawling and walking as she did for everything else, the sedate proceedings of the garden club could be totally disrupted. However, spring was a long time away, and anything could happen between now and then: a thought which inexorably reminded her of her date with Michael that evening, and of all the possible consequences.

In a chorus of affability she and the Darbys parted company, and Matthew drove her home. Work had piled up in her absence. She hauled on her old clothes and headed for the garage.

At suppertime Ashley was too nervous to eat very much. Afterwards she put Victoria to bed and had a long hot shower, drying her hair in her bedroom. She had already decided to wear her green plaid skirt with a beige silk blouse, and to leave her hair loose; under the skirt and blouse she wore a set of extravagantly lacy underwear. She splashed on perfume, and covered her pale cheeks with a liberal dousing of blusher. But no amount of make-up could hide the panic lurking in her grey eyes or the nervous tremor of her lips. Pulling on her mohair vest, and over it her coat, she went downstairs.

Exercising a diplomacy that must have cost him dearly, Matthew did not ask when she would be home or why she was going. Ostentatiously turning the pages of his book—which was about sheep-rearing, she noticed—he said, frowning at the page, 'Drive carefully. Got your key?'

She dropped a kiss on his wiry white hair, thinking how well its unmanageability expressed his whole personality. 'Yes. Don't wait up for me, will you?'

'Got no intentions of it.' He turned another page.

It seemed to take no time to cover the forty miles between the garage and Valleyview Farm; Ashley would have preferred the distance to have doubled. She wound up the driveway between the stark, skeletal trees, their tangled branches briefly illuminated by the headlights. At the top of the hill she parked the Honda beside the jeep, picked up her handbag, and got out of the car. Her heart was beating as rapidly as if she had just run up the hill rather than driven up it. The lights were on in the downstairs of Michael's wing. Slowly she started to walk towards it. *Mary Queen of Scots on her way to the scaffold . . .*

The front door burst open and a small red-haired boy catapulted on to the steps. 'Ashley!' he yelled. 'Guess what?'

Reprieve . . . 'What?' she responded obligingly.

He dashed across the gravel towards her. 'I found the instruction book for the tiller, so I greased and oiled it. Want to come and see?'

If she had been strictly truthful she would have answered, 'No,' for she was far too preoccupied with rehearsing what she was going to say to Michael to be interested in any kind of a grease job. But she was not so self-absorbed to miss the fact that Tim must have been watching from the house for her arrival; nor was she heartless enough to banish the shine of pride and pleasure from his grey eyes. 'Sure,' she said. 'Is it in the shed?'

He grabbed her hand, pulling her along. 'Same place as before. Mr Gault let me keep the key while I was working on it. He said it was my responsibility.'

The tiller, which was resting on clean newspaper spread on the shed floor, was immaculate; had it been hers, Ashley would not have had the heart to take it out in the garden and get mud all over it. Its red paint shone; even the tyre treads had been washed. Tim knelt down beside it. 'I tightened all the nuts and bolts. I greased the wheel shaft and the sliding linkage—in here, see? And I oiled the universal, the end of the yoke, and the throttle cable.'

'It should work like a charm next spring. You did a good job, Tim.'

'Mr Gault said I could use it in the garden in the summer. He says I can stay at Valleyview. I won't have to leave like Kevin did.'

What happened tonight would determine whether she also came to stay at Valleyview, and whether Tim became a part of her life, as Victoria was. Her throat tight, she said, 'I'm glad, Tim.' She ruffled his hair, smiling at him more naturally. 'I'd better go. Thanks for showing me.'

'I'll lock the shed.' Solemnly he pulled the key from the pocket of his jeans; it was attached to his belt by a ravelled piece of string. As he sneaked one last admiring glance at the tiller before switching off the light, Ashley felt her heart turn over with love for him. Somehow it seemed to make her proposal this evening all the more difficult, for so much depended on the results.

After Tim left her at the front door, she continued round to the side of the house and tapped on Michael's door. He did not answer immediately. She had raised her hand to knock again when he swung the door open and she was left standing on the step with her fist raised, feeling rather foolish. 'Hello,' she said with no great originality.

'Come in.'

He was wearing dark slacks with an open-necked grey shirt, the sleeves rolled up. He was not smiling, and the blue eyes were guarded. Forbiddingly so, thought Ashley. 'I'm sorry if I'm late,' she babbled, walking inside. 'Tim wanted to show me all the work he's done on the tiller, so I went over to the shed with him.'

'I see.'

What had happened to the laughing-eyed man of this morning, the swashbuckling rescuer of the maiden in distress? There was certainly no sign of him now. She said desperately, 'May I go through to the living room?'

'Of course. Let me take your coat. Can I get you a drink?'

'Please.' She passed him her coat, being very careful not to touch him. 'Maybe a sherry?'

He hung up her coat, ushered her into the living room and disappeared into the kitchen. Too restless to sit still, Ashley got up and wandered around the room, picking things up and putting them down again, leafing aimlessly through a magazine. Michael came back into the room, passed her the sherry she had requested, and said point-blank, 'Why are you here, Ashley?'

All the little speeches she had so painstakingly rehearsed fled from her mind, leaving it totally blank. 'I . . .'

'You must have a reason. I can hardly believe this is simply a pleasant social visit—not after the way we parted a couple of weeks ago.'

She felt the first touch of anger and went on the offensive. 'Why did you come to the garage this morning?'

'Answer my question first.'

She swallowed. 'I want you to make love to me, Michael.' There, she had said it.

There was a moment's stunned silence, then very carefully he put down his drink. '*What* did you say?'

'I said what you thought I said . . . will you, Michael?' Ashley took a hefty gulp of the sherry.

'Am I permitted to ask the reason behind this sudden request?' Michael said silkily. 'As you may recall, the last time I tried to make love to you, you were not exactly . . . co-operative.'

'Oh, do stop! You're not making this any easier——'

'What kind of a game are you playing, Ashley?'

'It's not a game!' As she curled her fingers around the fragile crystal stem of the glass, the remaining liquid quivered and shook. 'I've never been more serious in my life.'

'Then will you please explain to me why you walked in the door and made that extraordinary request?'

She gathered all her courage, put the glass down, and walked over to him, taking his hands in hers and looking up into his face. 'Do you still love me, Michael? You said you did. You said you wanted to marry me.'

His hands did not return her pressure. 'None of that has changed,' he said flatly.

She had crossed the first hurdle. Her eyes warmed and her mouth curved in a shy smile. 'I found something out yesterday. I realised that I love you too, Michael.'

Subconsciously she might have hoped that her words would make him seize her in his arms, and that then one thing would lead to another. She was not to be so lucky. However, he did grasp her fingers in his and say inconsequentially, 'Your hands are cold ... are you nervous?'

'Scared to death.' It was a relief to be able to admit it, and suddenly the words came tumbling out. 'I've really missed you the last few days, and I felt terrible about the way we parted. Then yesterday a man was buying gas and I thought for a minute it was you, and when I realised it wasn't I sat down and cried my eyes out—and that was when I realised I love you.'

Michael looked a little confused by this recitation. But his features were softening and a light was shining in his eyes. 'Say that again—just the last part.'

'I love you.'

'Will you marry me?'

Her face clouded. She did not answer him directly. 'Please try and understand what I want to say, Michael, and don't take it wrong.' Her lashes dropped. 'You already know I—I didn't like making love to David. I'm still afraid that somehow it was my fault, and that the same thing might happen again with you. I can't marry you until I know that it—until I'm sure ...'

He finished for her. 'Until you know it's different with me. Because it will be, Ashley, I promise you that.'

'But I can't marry you until I know! Don't you see? What if I married you and then we were miserable together?'

'So that's why you marched in tonight and announced that you wanted to make love ... it took a long time to get the truth out of you.'

'Don't laugh at me, Michael,' she said in a low voice.

'I'm not, Ashley. I think you're brave and beautiful and I love you so much it frightens me.' He pulled on her hands. 'Come along.'

'Where are we going?' she faltered.

'Into the bedroom. It's the usual place to make love.'

It was what she had wanted, wasn't it? She followed him across the carpet, her footsteps dragging in the pile. The curtains were drawn in his bedroom, rose-coloured curtains that shut out the winter's night. Michael closed the door behind them, then released her hand to go and switch on a light in the bathroom, partly closing the door so that only a soft diffused glow came into the bedroom. Ashley was still standing by the door, her hands hidden in the folds of her skirt, her eyes wideheld. He said forcefully, 'Ashley, it will be good with me, I swear that to you. I love you, and my one desire is to make you happy.'

She nodded, knowing he believed every word he was saying, wishing she could as easily believe them. 'I'm scared,' she gulped.

'I know you are.' He turned down the bed, and as naturally as if they had been sharing a room for months sat down on the end of it and pulled off his shoes and socks, then without haste took off his shirt, throwing it over the nearest chair. His body was beautiful, as economical in movement as it was elegant in structure, firmly muscled, light brown hair curling from breastbone to navel.

Ashley's predominant emotion was stark, unreasoning fear. She watched him get up and walk towards her. He stopped only a few inches away from her. Again as if it was something he had done many times before, he began undoing the small pearl buttons on her blouse. He must have felt her flinch, but ignoring her reaction, he took off her blouse, tossing it to join his shirt, then undid the waistband of her skirt. It fell to the floor in a rustle of silk lining. Automatically Ashley stepped out of it, slipping out of her shoes and of her own accord sliding her tights down her legs. *Now what,* she thought, panic-stricken. *Why did I ever come here? I must have been mad.*

She did not realise how expressively her eyes mirrored her thoughts. With a wordless exclamation Michael took her in his arms, kneading the rigid muscles of her spine in a gesture that was comforting rather than sexual. 'Don't look so frightened,' he murmured against her hair. 'I won't hurt you. Everything I do you will want me to do, I promise you that.' As if he sensed that it would take more than words to convince her, he released her long enough to unbuckle his belt and step out of his slacks. Leaving them in a heap on the floor, he led her over to the side of the bed, put his arms around her and kissed her.

She was trembling like a wild creature caught in a trap. His mouth was gentle, although very sure of itself; his hands soothed and stroked with infinite tenderness. Yet Ashley could not stop trembling. Her palms were pressed against his chest more to hold him away than from any desire for contact, and sickly, in her mind, she was beginning to wonder if David had not been right. It was she who was at fault, she who was unable to respond . . . *oh, Michael, Michael!*

He loosened his hold on her. Sitting down on the edge of the bed, he grasped her hands to pull her down with him. She found she could not meet his eyes. And so, unintentionally, her gaze fell, and for the first time she saw the knee that had been injured three years ago. The scars were white now, ugly and twisted; the surgeon's neatly stitched lines seemed horribly incongruous amid the torn, ridged flesh.

She remembered with sickening clarity how he had received the injury and had been left alone to die, and a tiny sound of distress was wrenched from her lips. She dropped to her knees beside him, impulsively pressing her cheek to the scarred flesh, her hair cascading over his thigh. Shining like precious stones, two tears dripped on to his knee.

'Ashley ... dear God, sweetheart, don't look like that!'

The barriers were down, her fears banished in the blinding flash of knowledge that so easily she might never have met Michael, might never have known the love that now flooded her body with an aching need to be close to him. Two more tears trickling down her cheeks, she blindly raised her face for his kiss.

His restraint was gone. His lips demanded all she had to give, and willingly, joyously, she gave it, opening to him, her nails digging into his shoulders. They fell back on the bed, his weight crushing her into the mattress, her hair spread like spun gold on the pillow. She felt against her thigh the imperative hardening of his groin, and involuntarily her hips moved to gather him in.

Michael raised his head, seeing the pagan glitter of desire in her eyes and the wash of colour across her cheekbones. Bringing his hand up, he deliberately cupped her breast, stroking it to its tip and hearing her moan with untutored pleasure. Just as deliberately he took off her two remaining garments and his own briefs, so that nothing barred the intimacy of their flesh; then, moving his hips against hers in slow, tantalising circles, he traced the pale, blue-veined flesh of her breast with his lips. For a few moments Ashley lay still, savouring the exquisite, agonising pleasure of that twin assault, wanting to laugh and cry, to sing and weep, wanting it to last forever yet to rush to its inevitable climax.

Sensing her stillness, Michael looked up, an expression in his eyes that she had never seen there before. In that single look was all his love, for he had opened his soul to her; it was his gift to her, that, and his body's homage. She whispered shakily, her eyes wet with unshed tears, 'I love you, Michael. I'm crying because I'm so happy.'

'I love you, too.' He kissed her again, a leisurely exploration that left her weak with longing. Wanting to give him some of the joy he was bringing her, she murmured, 'Tell me what to do, Michael. How can I please you?'

It never occurred to her that in those two small questions she was revealing the wasteland that her love affair with David had been. But she saw his face change, and said in sudden dismay, 'Shouldn't I have asked? Did I do wrong?'

'God, no.' He hesitated. 'I suddenly realised how very innocent you still are. I'm glad of that, Ashley, glad that I'll be the man to lead you into the many paths of love. Because you've never walked them before, have you?' He caressed her breasts, then let his hand move lower across the smooth expanse of her belly, and lower still, to where his thighs had her pinioned. Her indrawn breath was instinctive; her response rippled across her face, shocking her with its force and its fierce mingling of pain and pleasure.

Before she could become lost in her own tumultuous needs, whose existence she had only suspected until now, she begged again, 'I want to do something for you, Michael. To please you.'

'Then touch me.' He took her hand, guiding it the length of his body, so that she felt beneath her palm the roughness of hair, the smooth interplay of muscle and bone, and then, in the most intimate caress of all, the very centre of his manhood.

Words lost their meaning. The world dropped away. For Ashley there was only Michael and herself and their frantic need of each other; and as he entered her, the experiencing of a new, mysterious and all-powerful union that caught her up in its rhythms. She was flung into a land where she had never been before, and cried out his name again and again; as he throbbed within her, she lost herself in the burning blue fire of his eyes even as he was lost in her.

It could have been moments or minutes before she felt him lever himself up on his elbow, taking some of his weight off her. Dreamily she opened her eyes and said with naïve simplicity, 'I feel wonderful.'

'Good.' He smiled at her, a lazy smile full of complicity. 'So do I.'

It was a smile that was difficult to resist. However, there was something she very much wanted to say. Her brow wrinkled with thought, she said slowly, 'In a very real way, and despite Victoria's existence, I feel as though it's tonight that I've lost my virginity, or my innocence, or whatever you want to call it. With you, not with David. I never experienced anything like this with David. I want you to know that.'

'I knew it already, Ashley. But thank you for telling me.'

'You did?'

'I did. Do you want to know something else?'

'Yes,' she said promptly. 'Why did you come to the garage this morning after I phoned you?'

He laughed. 'That wasn't what I was going to tell you. I was going to tell you that as time goes on and we do this more often, we'll get better.'

'Impossible,' she said firmly.

'I'll take that as a compliment . . . I went tearing off to the garage because I couldn't stand staying at home wondering what you wanted.'

'Then why were you so—so cold and distant when I arrived this evening?'

'I'd convinced myself by then that you were going to tell me you never wanted to see me again. That the relationship was over. Ended.'

'I'd never have heard the last of it from Grandad if I'd done that!' she laughed.

'You know, I've been thinking of adding another wing at the back of the house,' Michael told her. 'Do you think Matthew would like to come and live here, too?'

'Too?' she queried demurely.

'As well as you. And Victoria. You will marry me, won't you, Ashley?'

'Yes.'

'I'd like to adopt Victoria.'

'Yes.'

'And Tim?'

'Yes.'

'And have a couple of children of our own?'

She laughed. 'This is getting monotonous! But again, yes. Are you sure you want Grandad as well?'

'If he'd like to come.'

'Probably. He was reading a book on sheep-rearing this evening when I left.'

'So how many's that?' asked Michael. 'Five, is it?'

'The way we've been carrying on, it could be six.'

'I'll get a special licence tomorrow. Because I'm the marrying kind, Ashley.'

'I know that ... maybe we should phone Grandad right now.'

Michael pulled her on top of him, so that her hair gleamed against his skin. 'Or maybe I should show you that it can be even better.'

To their mutual satisfaction he soon proved that he was right—it could be better. So it was midnight before Ashley phoned Matthew and told him he was invited to a wedding.

ANNE MATHER

Anne Mather, one of Harlequin's leading
romance authors, has published more
than 100 million copies worldwide,
including **Wild Concerto,**
a *New York Times* best-seller.

Catherine Loring was an
innocent in a South
American country beset by
civil war. Doctor Armand
Alvares was arrogant
yet compassionate.
They could not ignore
the flame of love igniting
within them...whatever
the cost.

HIDDEN IN THE FLAME

Share the joys and sorrows of real-life love with
Harlequin American Romance!™

Twice in a Lifetime
REBECCA FLANDERS

GET THIS BOOK
FREE as your introduction to Harlequin American Romance — an exciting series of romance novels written especially for the American woman of today.

Mail to:
Harlequin Reader Service

In the U.S.
2504 West Southern Ave.
Tempe, AZ 85282

In Canada
P.O. Box 2800, Postal Station A
5170 Yonge St., Willowdale, Ont. M2N 6J3

YES! I want to be one of the first to discover

Harlequin American Romance. Send me FREE and without obligation *Twice in a Lifetime*. If you do not hear from me after I have examined my FREE book, please send me the 4 new **Harlequin American Romances** each month as soon as they come off the presses. I understand that I will be billed only $2.25 for each book (total $9.00). There are no shipping or handling charges. There is no minimum number of books that I have to purchase. In fact, I may cancel this arrangement at any time. *Twice in a Lifetime* is mine to keep as a FREE gift, even if I do not buy any additional books.　　　　　154 BPA BPGE

Name   (please print)

Address   Apt. no.

City   State/Prov.   Zip/Postal Code

Signature (If under 18, parent or guardian must sign.)

This offer is limited to one order per household and not valid to current Harlequin American Romance subscribers. We reserve the right to exercise discretion in granting membership. If price changes are necessary, you will be notified.

AMR-SUB-1R

Harlequin

INDULGE IN THE PLEASURE OF SUPERB ROMANCE READING BY CHOOSING THE MOST POPULAR LOVE STORIES IN THE WORLD

Longer, more absorbing love stories for the connoisseur of romantic fiction.

An innovative series blending contemporary romance with fast-paced adventure.

Contemporary romances—uniquely North American in flavor and appeal.

and you can never have too much romance.